JACK CURTIS grew impatient with Peggy's rejection. He longed to make love to her, but she resisted his every advance. Would his bride ever share his bed?

PEGGY CURTIS rushed into marriage to bury the memory of that terrible night with Ron Becker. Now the touch of her husband revulsed her. Would she ever be able to show Jack how much she loved him?

JOANNA CURTIS had become a new woman right before Kay's eyes. It was no wonder that Kay took a special interest in her now. But Brock warned Joanna that there could be something unwholesome about Kay's feelings. Could he possibly be right?

———————————

Series Story Editor **Mary Ann Cooper** is America's foremost soap opera expert. She writes the nationally syndicated column *Speaking of Soaps*, is a major contributor to soap opera magazines, and has appeared on numerous radio and television talk shows.

Elizabeth Summers, author of *Far Side of Love*, is a freelance writer who lives in New York City. She has a passion for books, films, world trave

D1319603

Dear Friend,

Pioneer Communications Network takes great pride in presenting the eighth book in the Soaps & Serials paperback series. If this is your first Soaps & Serials book, you're in for a pleasant surprise. Our books give you a glimpse into the past, featuring some of the most exciting stories in the history of television soaps. For those of you who are old friends of the Soaps & Serials line, thanks for your support.

Here's one of the many questions we've received from our thoughtful and loyal fans. A reader from Des Plaines, Illinois, insists that Brenda Dickson is not the only actress who has played Jill Foster Abbott. Her friend claims that Brenda created the role. Who's right? Brenda did create the role but left the show for a while and was replaced by Deborah Adair. Brenda later resumed the role when Deborah left.

Although we can't answer all of the letters we receive, we still enjoy hearing from you. Keep writing!

For Soaps & Serials books,

Mary Ann Cooper

Mary Ann Cooper

P.S. If you missed previous Soaps & Serials books and can't find them in your local book source, please see the order form inserted in this book.

The Young and the Restless

8
FAR SIDE OF LOVE

William J. Bell and Lee Phillip Bell, Co-Creators,
Executive Producers, and Head Writers

Soaps™
& Serials

PIONEER COMMUNICATIONS NETWORK, INC.

Far Side of Love

THE YOUNG AND THE RESTLESS paperback novels are published and distributed by Pioneer Communications Network, Inc.

SOAPS & SERIALS™ is a trademark of Pioneer Communications Network, Inc.

ISBN: 0-916217-78-7

Printed in Canada

10 9 8 7 6 5 4 3 2 1

FAR SIDE OF LOVE

Chapter One

A Time for Love

Liz Foster stood at her bedroom window looking down onto the sweep of circular driveway, already lined with parked cars. A brilliant winter sun filtered through the bare trees as she watched Snapper and Greg, crisply handsome in their dark suits accented with white boutonnieres, graciously escort guests up the front porch and into the house. Snapper's hair was still slicked back, wet from the shower, and it reminded her of how he had looked as a youngster, reluctantly going off to school in the morning. Now her sons were grown men.

Liz shivered lightly as she pulled her thin cotton robe more tightly around her. The ceremony would start in an hour. She had to get dressed.

She imagined Bill was already downstairs mingling with their guests, greeting friends in his warm husky voice, clasping hands with his firm grip. Bill. It seemed incredible that after nine long years he was back in her life again, that in one short hour they would be husband and wife—again. She smiled to herself. Not every woman was lucky enough to have two wedding nights in one lifetime with the same wonderful man.

Liz took her dress from its padded hanger and gently eased it over her head. Her daughter Jill had wanted to help her get dressed, but she had wanted to be alone. It was one thing for a nervous young bride to be surrounded by attentive family. But Liz was no longer a child; she preferred to savor this moment in private, to be alone with her thoughts. She pulled the champagne-silk dress over her head and smoothed it down over her still slim hips; the delicately pleated bodice, dusted with tiny seed pearls, accented the gentle swell of her breasts. Sitting down at her vanity, she began to brush her hair, still thick and lustrous and barely streaked with gray. The last time she got married, she thought ruefully, there wasn't a gray hair in sight. But this time was even more precious.

When Bill had first come back, stricken with emphysema, she'd had to fight off the waves of pity that had welled up inside her, competing with feelings of anger and betrayal. He had left her and the children nine years ago, without thought or explanation. And suddenly she was expected to welcome him with open arms and nurse him back to health. Legally he was no longer even her husband, yet he seemed to expect to return to their lives—and her bedroom—as though nothing had happened.

But he had changed. His illness and gradual recovery had left him quieter, more gentle and tender. Thoughtful. Liz was glad she had insisted they sleep in separate bedrooms until they got married again. Maybe it would seem silly to some people, but to Liz it meant everything. She loved Bill, with every fiber of her being, and she wanted him with her always. Always. How long would that be? she thought with a sudden stab of fear. Now that he was back, enfolding her in his arms again, devouring her with the kisses she had pined for for nine years—how much time did they have?

With the care and attention of his family, Bill's health had improved. The coughing fits that racked his body had subsided, then disappeared altogether. The energy and life had returned to his muscular frame. But his illness was still there, lurking, casting a shadow on their happiness, their future.

Liz blotted her lips and shook her head slightly, as though to banish any such thoughts from her mind. This was her wedding day, she reminded herself, as she pinned a delicate spray of baby's breath and tiny yellow rosebuds into her hair. Cocking her head to one side, she examined her image appraisingly. Perhaps the flowers were too girlish a touch. No, she decided, and smiled to herself. Today was her wedding day, and she would be as girlish as she damn well pleased.

Snapper stood at the bottom of the curved staircase looking out over the guests milling around in the living room and chatting with subdued excitement. This was an event Genoa City had never expected to see, and everyone was eager to be part of it.

He looked at his watch nervously. In just eight minutes he would be escorting his mother downstairs and presenting her hand in marriage to his own father. He looked over and watched as Bill Foster moved from one group of their friends to another, touching a shoulder here, shaking a hand there, laughing and smiling that quiet, confident smile. Snapper had to admit it had been hard for him when his father had first come back home.

The pain had been almost unbearable when he'd

left nine years ago—a feeling of complete betrayal mixed with an almost childlike bewilderment. Snapper would never forget the sorrow that had etched his mother's face, and even after all this time, the hurt was still too fresh to forget or forgive easily.

Snapper caught his brother, Greg, and his younger sister, Jill, watching him from the other side of the living room, and their eyes met and held for a moment. They had become closer during this time, tightened their ranks as a family and learned how to lean on each other when they really needed to. They'd all been secretly relieved when their parents' marriage had been officially terminated because of the length of Bill's desertion. After nine years, Bill Foster was considered dead in the eyes of the law. At last the waiting and wondering were over; their mother was free to meet someone new and to love again.

Her willingness to take Bill back when he appeared on her doorstep, sick and weak, to nurse him back to health, had been a source of confusion and anger. They loved their father—but how could they possibly turn back the clocks and pretend nothing had changed?

"I will never love a man the way I love your father," Liz had declared, almost angrily, when she'd gathered them together to announce her wedding plans. "He needs me now, and I've never stopped needing him. I want to have your blessing, but even if I don't, I will go ahead with the wedding anyway."

Snapper had been the one to say out loud what they had all been thinking. "Mother," he'd said gently, "even though he's made a remarkable recovery, he's still a very sick man. We know you love him—we love him, too—but are you sure you understand the possible burden you might be taking on? What if he has a relapse and needs constant care? You're still a young woman, and you don't owe him the best years of your life. He didn't give you his," he added quietly, his voice sharp with bitterness.

"You are my children and I love you with all my heart," she said proudly. "But he is my husband, and I will give him everything I have to give—until death do us part."

Jennifer Brooks leaned over the buffet table in the dining room and added a few last sprigs of parsley and watercress to the platters that were already laid out for the reception following the ceremony. Liz had wanted to hire a caterer, but Jennifer had insisted that this wasn't the kind of occasion when you wanted strangers around. She and her daughters had worked hard, and the results were certainly worth it, she thought with a thrill of pride as she eyed the magnificent spread. There was a whole salmon elegantly garnished with thinly sliced cucumber, tiny finger sandwiches, duck liver and truffle mousse, glistening roast turkey and ham, and her pièce de résistance —the wedding cake, a four-tiered confection decorated with delicate silver-white bells and paper doves with minuscule wings.

It had been important to Jenifer to make this wedding a special occasion for Liz and Bill. Perhaps because she herself was feeling the passage of time so keenly; was so aware of the importance of living each moment to the fullest. She looked over to where her daughters were discussing last-minute arrangements with Liz's daughter, Jill, and felt her eyes prick with tears.

The mastectomy had been hell to endure. But it

wasn't losing her breast that bothered her so much as the increasing bouts of exhaustion, the feeling that she no longer had the energy to keep up with the pace of her life. If it weren't for her family—their problems, their energy, their love, and most especially her husband, Stuart—she wouldn't be able to keep going.

And moments like this. Maybe it was sentimental, but to her Liz and Bill's wedding seemed like a gift of life itself. Their willingness to begin again, even when life itself seemed to be waning, was what counted. She thought of the tickets that were folded in her small leather handbag. Liz and Bill had planned to spend their honeymoon at home in Genoa City. Jennifer and her husband had wanted to give them a special gift and decided on a trip to Hawaii. It was almost as though this wedding were for them, the kind of starting over they wished they could have.

But could anyone buy time? Jennifer wondered. Frowning thoughtfully, she made the final adjustments to several clusters of purple, red and green grapes that spilled out of a silver filigreed bowl, then stepped back to survey her handiwork.

Could she?

Joanna couldn't help staring over at the buffet, wondering what the food was going to be like—even though she wasn't going to have a thing except a few carrot sticks, she reassured herself hastily. It was second nature, and it was hard to break the habit of a lifetime, she thought defensively. Even though she was down to a slinky size-eight dress these days, her head and her stomach still had a mind of their own. Joanna smoothed the peach shirtwaist dress over her hips and tossed her hair back over her shoulders. She knew she looked great these days and just hoped that her ex-husband was taking a good look at what he was missing.

She had spotted Jack as soon as she'd walked into the Fosters' home, the way she always did. From the moment she'd first met Jack Curtis, she'd been drawn to him like a magnet. When he'd lost interest in her, she had tried to forget him and find someone else. She had tried to convince herself that all her hard work dieting was for herself—and herself alone. But it was no use—his image would always be with her, floating in the back of her mind. Would Jack like this dress? Would Jack approve?

For a moment, she felt her confidence waver as she watched Jack bend over to listen and laugh at some comment Peggy was making. Why on earth did Peggy Brooks have to come into his life, anyway? she thought with the old helpless anger. They didn't make nearly the couple she and Jack did—and they never would. But what did she care? She was young, and now she was beautiful. There were plenty of other men. And she was going to find one of them —soon.

Liz jumped at the soft knock on the bedroom door. Jolted out of her reverie, she glanced at her tiny diamond-studded watch, an extravagant gift from Bill. It was almost time. She opened the door and stood looking at Snapper for a long moment. This time the tears welled up in her eyes. She would smudge her eye makeup, but so what? Makeup could always be repaired. A moment like this happened once in a lifetime, and then only if you were lucky. They embraced long and hard and silently. Finally

Snapper stepped back, holding his mother's hands in his.

"You make a beautiful bride, Mrs. Foster," he said huskily.

"And you, Dr. Foster, make a beautiful escort," she replied, smiling through her tears. "What other woman has had the privilege of being given away in marriage to her own husband by her own handsome grown-up son?" Giving a final swift look around her bedroom—their bedroom, she corrected herself—she felt a moment of panic.

She squeezed her son's arm tightly. "I am doing the right thing, aren't I, Snap?" she whispered, unconsciously using the childhood diminutive. "I'm not making a mistake, am I? . . .

"No," she said firmly, answering her own question. "I'm ready. Let's go downstairs." /

Kay Chancellor sometimes felt as if she'd spent her whole life at weddings and funerals. But this occasion had its unique qualities, she had to admit. Liz Foster had looked beautiful walking down the stairs on Snapper's arm, every inch the radiant bride. No, that had to be wrong. What did you call brides the second time around—and to the same man? Secondhand Rose, she thought, and then felt ashamed of her cynicism.

Ever since the death of her husband, the discovery of his affair right before his death and the bitterness surrounding the custody suit for *his* child, not theirs, Kay had had a hard time *not* being cynical. When she wasn't drinking—and she had been trying hard lately and succeeding—she seemed to need to hide behind that armor of toughness. If you didn't let anything get to you, then it couldn't hurt you: that had become her motto. She couldn't suddenly change her outlook just because two old friends were marching down the aisle again. So why had she gotten so choked up when the justice of the peace had declared them man and wife and Bill had taken Liz in his arms for a long, passionate, oblivious-to-the-world kiss? Kay, old girl, she thought, you're still a sentimental sap at heart.

The Foster wedding had decided Jack Curtis on one thing. He was ready to get married. Tomorrow was too late, as far as he was concerned. He looked protectively down at Peggy as she held on to his arm with one long, delicate, elegantly manicured hand. He wasn't going to put up with her excuses and her stalling anymore. Naturally it had taken her a long time to recover from the shock of the rape; he understood that. But life had to go on, and as far as he was concerned the best thing for her would be to marry him and begin their life together. By putting it off, she simply allowed herself to remain in a limbo state that invited memories of the past. He longed to be able to take her in his arms and brush away those memories as though they were cobwebs. He could always tell by the look in her eyes when he had lost her, when she was traveling back to that horrifying night and reliving every moment of it. When he tried to reach out to bring her back, she recoiled.

"Don't touch me!"

"But honey, it's only me—Jack. Let me hold you."

"Don't touch me!" she repeated over and over in a kind of cold monotone, as though she could not see beyond the movie reel that rolled inexorably inside her own head.

Thankfully, those times had gotten fewer and

farther between. But even so, they remained as a barrier between them—a time bomb that could explode at any moment. Jack had felt helpless, and sometimes angry.

"How do you expect to live your life like this? You can't go on hiding forever. I know I can't understand, *really* understand, what you've been through," he said tightly, hating the sarcasm he heard in his own voice. "But you have to let someone try to help you sometime. You can't go on living with this nightmare forever. I want to help you. I'm *trying* to help you, but you have to let me in."

She had sat, her face pale and set, her hands twisted into a knot of tension and resistance. Jack had turned on his heel and stormed out; later, after he had jumped into his car and gone hurtling out of the driveway and onto the street, he wished he had held his temper in check and tried to coax her back. But a man had his limits.

Today, though, she looked at peace, he thought hopefully, as though she had reached some kind of inner decision. He hoped it was the decision he wanted—*needed*—to hear. Tonight he would ask her to marry him.

Liz had never been to Hawaii before. When she opened the envelope that read "With all our love and best wishes for the future, Jennifer and Stuart Brooks," she had to swallow an almost impossibly large lump in her throat. Sometimes the thought of what they all lived with seemed impossible to bear. Happiness was so fleeting! Here she and Bill were being offered a romantic wedding trip to Maui, and all she really wanted to do was stay in Genoa City among her friends and family. To get up in the morning in her own kitchen and make scrambled eggs and coffee for her husband—that was honey-moon enough for her.

She also had to admit that she was scared. They would only be gone for four days, but what if something happened? Of course they had hospitals in Hawaii, and besides, Bill had made such a total recovery—why was she so scared? Probably because dealing with illness and the possibility of death made you appreciate that life was really made up of the small moments, not the lavish extravagances and glamorous times. She didn't need Hawaii. She had Bill.

But Bill had seemed so pleased. They would go. They would walk on the beach and be totally alone in a wonderful balmy paradise. The gentle warm air would be marvelous for Bill's lungs. It would be a renewal—they would return to Genoa City, strengthened in mind and body, ready to pick up the threads of their lives. Everything would work out, she said to herself for the hundredth time. It had the sound of a prayer.

Kay was amazed by the transformation that Joanna had undergone. She hadn't seen her since, oh, probably since her waitressing days, and the change was really remarkable. If only she would learn how to dress. The dress she was wearing was obviously brand new and did nothing for her figure and color-ing.

Kay found herself next to Joanna at the buffet, both reaching for the Perrier bottle at the same time.

"I can see we have the same good habit," Kay said drily, filling Joanna's glass with a flourish and then topping up her own. "You know, if it weren't for Perrier, I don't know how I'd get through these occasions."

Joanna laughed. "If it weren't for carrot and celery sticks, I don't know how I'd get through, either."

A sweet little thing, Kay mused. But she obviously needed some guidance. Maybe she should try to help her out a little, go shopping with her and get her to stop using that vile blue eye shadow. Why did so many women use that awful stuff? Maybe to pretend their high school prom wasn't that far behind. But it certainly was unbecoming. Now Liz looked every inch her age—and every inch of it earned and beautiful. Joanna was young yet, but it wouldn't hurt for her to take a lesson from Liz in the elegance of aging well. For that matter, maybe I need a few lessons, too, she thought sardonically. Here I am, alone again, not a soul to spend my time or my money on. Maybe Joanna would be as good a place to start as any. My little Pygmalion. Her mouth curved in a small secret smile as she sipped her Perrier and allowed Joanna's chatter to flow over her.

Driving home from the Fosters' wedding, Jack was grateful that he remembered the little out-of-the-way restaurant; it enabled him to casually suggest a late supper, as though he'd thought of it on the spur of the moment. He was nervous as he pulled into the parking lot and ushered Peggy into one of the polished-wood booths lit softly by a small, amber-globed table lamp. The place had the kind of quiet warmth that, along with a glass of Bordeaux, could warm anyone up. He was hoping it would work some magic on Peggy.

Strange, he mused. It was here he had proposed to his wife, Joanna. His *ex*-wife, Joanna. They had stopped in for a sandwich after a long fall ride, and the words had simply fallen from his mouth, unplanned. She had been so happy and immediately moved over to join him on his side of the booth, as though the distance of the table between them were too much.

Joanna had been a sweet kid. For a fleeting moment he wished it was she sitting across the table—chattering aimlessly and making her ingenuous whispered comments about other people in the restaurant—instead of this beautiful, intense, tormented woman. Yet he loved Peggy, wanted to possess her completely, to give her the kind of protection and safety and passion that would make her flower into a complete woman again. And he had a sense of urgency about it, as though continuing to wait patiently might be disastrous. Suddenly he felt shy, tongue-tied. It was hard to know where to begin.

It ended up being surprisingly easy. All he needed to say was, "Peggy, I've been thinking . . ." for her to cover his hands with hers and say:

"Yes, Jack, I know. I've been thinking, too."

Their plans seemed to be made in a matter of minutes. It would be a quiet private ceremony with only a witness, no friends or family. They would drive up for a long weekend to a small but beautiful country inn that Jack had been to a number of years before. There they would have time alone together and be able to return to Genoa City without a lot of questions from curious friends and family.

It had been wonderful to see Liz and Bill surrounded by well-wishers and loved ones, but at the same time it had filled Peggy with a feeling of panic. Getting married wasn't something to be frightened of, she knew; it's what she had wanted for so long. But ever since the rape, even the smallest and most meaningless of events had taken on momentous significance. Getting in the car and going shopping seemed fraught with potential danger. What if the car got stuck on the highway? What if she was attacked by a shoplifter in the store? More often than not, she would opt to stay home in the safety of her bedroom, where nothing could happen.

But with the warmth of a glass of vintage Bordeaux, the golden light of the tiny roadside restaurant and Jack's eyes so gentle and loving on her, the future seemed bright and filled with hope—not at all threatening. Maybe she could forget the nightmare and be happy again. She squeezed Jack's hands between her own and said the simple word that had been so hard to say.

"Yes."

It had been so long since Liz had felt sand between her toes and the gentle whisper of tropical breezes on her flesh that she felt she must be dreaming. When she and Bill had arrived from the airport to their hotel, they were taken to a thatched cottage on the beach, nestled between palm trees and secluded from the rest of the world. A bottle of chilled Dom Pérignon waited for them in a silver ice bucket. A bowl of exotic fruits—mangoes, kiwi and pineapples—filled the air with a sweet spicy scent. A bamboo-framed bed beckoned invitingly from beneath a bower of fresh flowers. And outside, the whisper of the waves lapped at the shore.

Liz had stripped off her clothes and taken a hot shower with a jasmine-scented soap. Refreshed and relaxed, she'd slipped a flowing, red-flowered caftan —a gift from Jill—over bare silken skin and left her feet free. Then they'd carried their glasses of champagne out to the beach and strolled by the light of the moon, which reflected off the water in a rippled sheen of silver ice. Now, as she dug her toes deep into the talcum-soft sand, she tried to convince herself that this was real.

They stood facing each other, linked elbows and solemnly sipped champagne in the time-honored romantic gesture, and then burst out laughing. Bill swung Liz off the ground and twirled her around and around so that the red silk of her caftan rippled sensuously against her skin. Liz's doubts about the advisability of the trip disappeared. The balmy air seemed to be working wonders on Bill. Everything would be fine. Hours later, as she drifted off to sleep, she tried to remember when she had last felt such contentment. Probably never, she thought sleepily. Definitely never.

The pain in Bill's chest tightened in that old familiar knot. He tried to keep his breathing even, but the weight of his wife's head on his chest seemed to grow heavier with each long, steady breath she took. Sweat began to bead on his forehead and chest and trickle down onto the sheets. The bright tropical moonlight sent a shaft of light across the bedcovers, twisted from their hours of lovemaking. Was that what had caused the onset of this attack? Was he never going to be able to make love to his wife fully and completely, without having to pay for it?

Slowly he eased out from under Liz's arm and tiptoed to the bathroom. He closed the door and leaned heavily against it, staring at himself in the bathroom mirror. A thoughtful maid had placed two exotic blossoms in one of the water glasses on the back of the toilet. They seemed to mock him. He pressed a towel against his mouth to muffle the sound of his suddenly labored breathing. So much for this young newlywed, he thought.

Chapter Two

The Burden of Silence

Liz pushed through the swinging doors of the hospital and headed for the front desk. The two nurses behind the desk nodded a sympathetic hello, but she walked past them without noticing. She had become a familiar figure at Genoa General in the last months.

Her days had fallen into a strange routine ever since the evening Bill had collapsed and was rushed to the hospital and admitted to intensive care. The four blissful days in Hawaii seemed to belong to some other woman; a kaleidoscope of colorful memories—picnics on the beach, sun-kissed days of splashing in waterfalls like a couple of children, nights filled with long, tender lovemaking—all seemed like some crazy dream. How could Bill have appeared so healthy, so back to his old self, only to collapse just two weeks after they'd returned from their honeymoon? Had he been hiding the truth from her all that time? Had he been secretly in pain but unwilling to spoil her happiness? Damn the man if that was true. That wasn't what loving was all about.

"Mom!" Lost in thought, Liz didn't falter in her steps until a hand reached out and grabbed her elbow.

"Snapper," she said dully, and continued to walk down the long hospital corridor toward intensive care.

"Mom, what are you doing back here? You promised you'd go home and get some rest. Dad's condition is stable. There's nothing you can do here, and we all need you to keep up your strength. I promised I would call you if anything changed."

For a moment Snapper's words seemed to register, and a look of pain and exhaustion crossed her face. Then, as though a shutter had closed, her face went blank again.

Snapper sighed with frustration, banging his clipboard against his leg. How could he reach her? The contrast of a few weeks of intense happiness followed by Bill's sudden relapse was obviously too much for her. He should have stepped in and advised them not to go to Hawaii. His better instincts had told him to do so on the day of the wedding. Knowing his father, he was sure the man had bent over backward to hide any attacks from her. And there was no telling how much pain he had endured alone. A fool in paradise. There were times when male pride really didn't help anyone.

"Dr. Foster," blared the intercom. "Paging Dr. Foster."

"Damn," Snapper muttered. Gently he took his mother by the elbow and walked with her to the waiting room off the intensive care unit. Telling her what to do wasn't going to make a bit of difference. She had already insisted on staying overnight at the hospital more than once in order to be near her husband, and stepping in and playing doctor, laying down the law, was only going to make her more stubborn. He'd have to work on a different angle.

Maybe if Greg or Jill came in and took over their mother's vigil, she would feel free enough to go home and sleep. It didn't seem enough to her that he, Snapper, was around the hospital, able to be with his father at a moment's notice. She wanted someone to be right there with Bill all the time, even when he was sleeping.

All that life-support equipment scared her to death, but when she stood at Bill's bedside she seemed to ignore it, as though it had nothing to do with sustaining her husband's life, as though her smile and touch alone kept him alive. And maybe she was right. She seemed to be reserving all of her strength for those moments by Bill's bed, to give him every ounce she had to offer, leaving nothing for herself.

Snapper was worried; they all were. She had been maintaining her solitary vigil for six months now. That kind of strength couldn't last forever.

Jill Foster hated hospitals. When she was a little girl and her parents took her for a check-up or a vaccination, just the smell of a hospital was enough to make her run back outside and dig her heels into the ground. Her mother and father had concocted elaborate schemes involving beautiful dolls, candy and other cherished treats, but the bribes had never really worked. Taking her to the hospital had always been a dreaded chore. Thank God they had never needed to do it too often.

Now she felt as though the antiseptic smell of the hospital would never leave her nostrils. At night, after a visit to the intensive care unit, she scrubbed and scrubbed her face and hands as though trying to wash away the nameless fear that illness and death aroused. But this feeling couldn't be washed away with Yardley's English Lavender. This was her own father lying there, hooked up to all those cold, frightening machines with their dials and monitors. When she first saw him lying in bed, so still and white, she'd had the urge to throw herself on him and cry, "Daddy! Daddy!" This couldn't be happening—not now, not when they'd only so recently become a family again. It just wasn't fair.

Jill pulled a tense hand through her mane of hair and raised the collar of her raincoat as though to shield herself from the ordeal ahead. Snapper had called and asked her to come in and take over their mother's watch—how could she say no? But she had wanted to; wanted to stay away and hide until it was all over. It seemed as though it were only yesterday that she had been back in that same hospital, watching the life of her beloved new husband slowly slip away, even as their unborn child moved in her belly. Now she had another death to face, and she just didn't know if she could handle it.

She had been pacing the halls for what seemed like hours, trying to avoid looking into other patients' rooms, trying to avoid the sight of illness all around her—an impossibility. She ended her cycle each time by stopping inside her father's private room. He looked so still and white, she thought, almost dead . . . and in a panic she raced to his bedside. No, the breathing was there, shallow, but there.

Sighing with relief—relief mixed with a kind of fury—Jill stamped down to the front waiting room and defiantly asked a man sitting there for a cigarette. After taking a few short, furious puffs, she stamped out the cigarette impatiently. What good would it do her father to kill herself?

Shoving her hands deeply into her pockets, she began to pace the halls once more. As she entered what she thought was her father's room, she suddenly stopped short, realizing she had made a mistake. Propped up in bed in front of her, his eyes bandaged, was a dark-haired man whose powerful build seemed to dwarf the bed, turning it into something from a child's nursery. She gasped and mumbled a quick excuse. But as she turned to leave, the man spoke.

"Please wait," he said, his voice cracking as though he hadn't spoken to anyone in hours. Slowly Jill turned around, walked over to the man's bed and stopped, looking down at him. Broad shoulders strained against the seams of his hospital gown. Strong, gentle hands rested lightly on either side of his body, palms open. There was a sense of both peace and strength about him that drew Jill, whose nerves were stretched to the breaking point, like a flower to the sun.

"Hi, I'm David Mallory. Who are you?" he asked with a slow smile, reaching out his hand in the direction of her voice. She moved close enough to take it and received a strong, warm handshake.

"My n-name is Jill . . . Jill Foster." She stumbled slightly over her words. "I'm here visiting my father —he's down the hall in intensive care. He has emphysema, and slips in and out of conciousness. My mother likes to have someone here when he's awake. So that's why I'm here." Jill felt foolish, like a tongue-tied young girl, in front of this man. Even though he couldn't possibly see her through the bandages, she found herself blushing, wondering how she looked.

"You have a lovely voice—and hands. I expect you're a very beautiful woman. Do you mind if I touch your face?"

The question came as a surprise, but for some reason Jill didn't mind the intimate request. She trusted this man instantly, something that she had rarely, if ever, experienced with a man. He reached out his hand, the fingers spread apart, and she bent closer. He touched her face with his fingertips, starting with a stroking motion over her hair and forehead, then skimming her eyes, nose and mouth and ending with her chin cupped in his hand. "Yes, a very beautiful woman." He smiled, showing a set of strong white teeth.

Suddenly Jill was so tired of hospital beds and sick people that she wanted to scream. David felt the sudden tension in her body.

"Is anything wrong? Did something just happen?"

"No," she said in a tight, angry voice, knowing she was acting childishly. "It's just that I'm so tired of sick people and I want to know what's wrong with your eyes, but part of me doesn't want to know at all. I'm sorry if that sounds rude, but I can't help it."

David let out a warm, rumbling laugh from somewhere deep in his chest. "It sounds perfectly sensible to me. I hate hospitals myself. I'm in here because I need a cornea transplant. I'm sitting around here waiting for a suitable donor. The only problem is, there are a lot more of us guys sitting out here waiting than there are corneas on the market. But I'm optimistic."

"Does that . . . mean . . . ." Jill couldn't bring herself to say the words.

"That I'm blind?" David finished almost cheerfully. "No, not quite. Yet, that is. But I will be if I don't get the operation soon." The warm smile faded and the beautifully sculpted mouth became pinched. "I just hope to God I get lucky."

Impulsively, Jill reached out and squeezed his hand. "I think you'll get lucky. I just have that feeling," she said, surprised at her own passionate response. What did she know about this stranger, this David Mallory? He meant no more to her than any other sick person lying in the hospital beds up and down the hall. But in her heart she knew that wasn't true. She had known him for perhaps fifteen minutes, and already he had become a part of her life.

Joanna wasn't used to luxury. When she was married to Jack they had lived off his salary as a college professor and her earnings as a waitress. Then she had started college herself, and things had gotten even tighter. Living on a shoestring had been a way of life. Now, all of a sudden, she was right smack in the very lap of luxury—and loving every minute of it.

When Kay Chancellor's son, Brock, had come to visit her the day after the Fosters' wedding, Joanna wasn't quite sure what to make of his suggestion.

"My mother's lonely, Joanna," he had said to her almost pleadingly. "I worry about her living alone, and drinking too much sometimes," he'd added softly. "I know you have trouble making ends meet, being in school and all that. She was telling me how much she enjoyed talking to you at the wedding reception, what a sweet girl you are, and I was thinking maybe it would be a good idea if you could move in with her for a while, be her roommate. It's not like she needs a baby-sitter or anything, just someone to keep her company. And life could be a little easier on you, cutting down on expenses."

When Joanna had opened her mouth to respond,

Brock had raised one hand to silence her. "No, I want you to think this over carefully, Joanna. Don't come to a snap decision."

If Brock could only know just how "snap" her decision was, Joanna laughed gleefully to herself later as she unpacked her two small suitcases and attempted to fill the large matching oak bureau and wardrobe in her elegantly appointed new bedroom. "More like a boudoir," she crowed to herself, taking a running jump and diving into the middle of the king-sized bed covered with a lush tapestried spread. With a pang she remembered the bed that she and Jack had bought when they'd first gotten married. They had paid for it over time, and it had only been a modest little double bed on a metal frame—but at the time it had seemed like the most luxurious thing in the world.

As usual, Joanna had to force all thoughts of Jack and Peggy out of her mind. She had heard that they were going to get married this week. Well, let them. She was living the good life now, and Peggy was welcome to scrounge along as the wife of an English professor. As for herself, she wanted no part of it.

She looked in her closet and contemplated the new additions to her wardrobe. Kay Chancellor certainly had expensive taste. And she wasn't about to complain. The charcoal-gray suit with its tuck-waisted jacket and long, sleek skirt had cost almost as much as her college tuition for one semester! But Kay hadn't even glanced at the price tag. Joanna had peeked at it while she'd had her back turned busily selecting blouses to accompany the suit. She'd tried to stifle her gasp and had missed Kay's amused smile.

Oh, yes, Kay had thought, she had a live one on her hands. This young thing was like molding putty

—and pretty putty at that. She hadn't enjoyed shopping like this in years. Her own interest in clothes had diminished. But all this was a little like being a fairy godmother to a Cinderella—or was she really the wicked stepmother in disguise? Kay had laughed to herself—a deliciously sinful laugh—and had taken out her wallet.

She would take Joanna to dinner at Le Bistro. Teaching her about food was going to be an even bigger challenge than the clothes. As far as she could tell, Joanna's idea of a great dinner was a well-done minute steak and frozen peas. Maybe the lesson should begin with a dozen snails and a bottle of chilled Chardonnay. Yes, that would be very nice for the first lesson. And how nice that there were so many more to come.

As a child, Peggy Brooks had dreamed of what her wedding would be like. She and her sisters had dressed up in elaborate combinations of slips and veils and taken turns being the bride and the bridesmaids. Once they had even convinced Greg and Snapper to act as groom and best man, but they had jeered at the game and ruined it.

The five-minute ceremony in the town clerk's office wasn't at all what she had dreamed. She wore a simple winter-white suit and carried two delicate white rosebuds that Jack had presented to her that morning with an appropriately romantic quote from *Romeo and Juliet*. Peggy had blushed and thanked him, but nevertheless she now felt a sense of disappointment, of emptiness. Hadn't she always wanted to get married in a church, with soaring organ music and a choir? Where was the reception and the dancing? There was something almost sneaky about this, about the two of them saying their vows in this stark office. And why couldn't she get rid of the knot in her stomach that gripped her each time she thought about the night to come—her wedding night?

She knew Jack would be gentle. When he embraced her, it was carefully, delicately, as though he were holding a rare antique that might drop to the ground and shatter. Peggy appreciated his care and his concern. But it also made her self-conscious, aware of her fears, as though they were being guarded too carefully. Would it be easier if he had crushed her to him and simply taken her to bed, insisting that they make love before taking their wedding vows? Was that what she had secretly longed for? Not the tortured violation of a rape, but a strong, passionate possession by the man she loved? And yet she did shrink from his touch.

What did she want?

The Wayside Inn was an intimate lovers' hideaway nestled between lush, rolling hills, and the ride up was beautiful—and mostly silent. Once in a while, Jack would reach over and take her hand, squeezing it reassuringly. Unaccountably, this annoyed her; she wished he would just leave her alone. Obviously he was anticipating their wedding night as eagerly and as nervously as she. But what did he have to fear? He hadn't experienced the tearing pain, the overwhelming humiliation, when her virginity had been savagely ripped from her against her will. No, *that* little adventure was hers alone to deal with.

Peggy thrust thoughts of that evening from her mind and concentrated on the lulling ride and breath-taking scenery. She had bought a beautiful new negligee to wear that night, a filmy froth of lace that looked as though it would tear if you breathed on it. It had cost a fortune, but she figured if she couldn't have a proper wedding, then she would at least splurge on one magnificent nightgown.

When she'd brought home the expensive-looking box tied with a pink satin bow, she'd unwrapped it and blushingly showed the gown to her mother and father. Jennifer had exclaimed and jumped up to hug her. But her father had simply looked at it, a muscle twitching in his cheek, and said quietly, "It's beautiful, sweetheart." The sadness in his voice had caused her to burst into tears.

"What's wrong, Daddy?" she'd cried, dropping the nightgown and running to him.

"Nothing, sweetheart," he'd said, making an obvious effort to brighten up. "I guess I was just feeling sad that I wasn't going to be there to give my little girl away. But you're all grown up now."

A torrent of feeling had overcome her and she'd sobbed in her father's arms as he'd stroked her hair. All the years of hope and longing, the fantasizing about the man she would love and marry—all that had been shattered in ten minutes of irrevocable violation. Her father couldn't help her through this next hurdle, either.

"I'll be fine, Daddy," she had said in a tiny voice, muffled against his chest. "I'll be fine."

She remembered those brave words now as Jack pulled into the entranceway of the charming two-story inn. They got out and stretched, taking deep breaths of clean country air tinged with the pungent smell of smoke from the fireplace. They had two hours before their dinner reservations. More than anything, Peggy just wanted to sit in front of the fireplace, drink a brandy and hold hands with Jack. But she could feel his impatience, see the message in his eyes. We have waited long enough. Now is the time.

The delicate breast of pheasant garnished with braised leeks tasted like so much cardboard in Peggy's mouth. She reached for her wineglass and raised it carefully to her trembling lips, glancing covertly at Jack as she did so. He was methodically stabbing at his food and chewing without tasting. His jaw muscle continued to work even after he'd stopped chewing. His eyes were dull with a passion that had worked its way through disappointment and frustration to a smoldering fury.

They had both tried. Jack had been gentle and tender, had given her time alone and then removed her lacy nightgown as though she were a precious flower. But she could feel everything inside her recoil at his touch. His fingers had been like sharp needles, piercing her skin. When his hand had touched her breast, she'd flinched and clutched her nightgown to her.

"I can't, Jack, I can't!" had been all she could say.

The familiar dull flush had appeared on his cheeks, and she'd become frightened. She had tried his patience, and now that she was his wife, she saw he was determined to help her get over her fears. The terror in her had risen. When he'd moved to pull the nightgown away from her, the scream had welled up inside and forced its way out as though it had a life of its own. Soon there'd been a knock at the door and a discreet question from the hotel manager as they'd sat, frozen, on either side of the bed. Then slowly, as though making some final decision, Jack had risen to his feet and begun to dress.

"I'll see you down at dinner. Half-past seven,"

he'd said woodenly, and left the room. Peggy had jumped up and run over to the door to lock it behind him. Only then had she let go with a torrent of feeling—anger, pain, disappointment—that had been filling her chest, threatening to choke her. She didn't blame Jack for being angry. He had been patient with her for months. She had agreed to be his wife. And now, because of her, their honeymoon was a disaster. She poured out her grief into her pillow, soaking through the delicately embroidered case. Then she rose wearily and ran a bath, her thoughts flitting to home all the while. She was safe at home. That's where she wanted to be. Not here, not in this strange place with a man who had become a stranger.

Sighing, she slid into the bathtub and closed her eyes, feeling the heat soak into her, lessening the fear. She had made her decision.

Downstairs, Jack Curtis sat on a stool at the small polished-wood bar and ordered his third cognac. He had tossed the first one back, and it had hit him like a knife in the gut. Exactly what he'd wanted. The second one had suffused him with a numbing glow. That, too, was fine. Finally, as he began to sip his third drink, he felt the fury in him begin to subside. It wasn't Peggy's fault, but he couldn't help feeling betrayed. Suddenly his marriage, and their future, looked like one colossal bad joke. How were they supposed to continue a marriage when his simplest touch made her scream?

Later, as he and Peggy sat across from one another at dinner, Jack's thoughts turned suddenly to Joanna, to their wedding night. He remembered her soft eagerness, her shyness, her complete lack of embarrassment about her inexperience. She had been a willing pupil, yearning to be touched and taught

—everything. He had been a fool to think that simply putting a ring on Peggy's finger would help her to regain her trust in men. The scars of the rape went too deep for that. Maybe there had been scars before the rape, and the violence of the act had simply driven those fears into some unreachable corner of her unconscious.

Giving up on his pheasant, Jack let his hands fall to his lap and looked over at his new wife. "Peggy," he said gently. "It's all right. I'm sorry. It's all right. I'll take you home." When she looked up, he saw a small, frightened child. "I'll take you home," he repeated soothingly.

The honeymoon was over.

Wearily, Liz counted change from her purse and then carried her tray to one of the Formica tables in the hospital cafeteria. Shrugging out of her coat, she looked with distaste at the cherry Danish inside its plastic wrap. She felt as though she had tried to choke down just about every pastry Genoa General had to offer. It had been weeks since she'd been on the scale. Things like weight seemed so silly and unimportant right now, but the skirt she had put on this morning hung loosely about her hips and she knew she was looking gaunt. None of it really mattered, though, she thought wearily. Even when Bill was awake enough, she knew he couldn't really see her, let alone care what she looked like.

The day before, he had come to for a few minutes while she was standing beside his bed. She'd felt her heart begin to pound as his eyes had fluttered open. His words had come out in short, breathless gasps.

"Liz . . ." he'd whispered so faintly that she'd had to stoop to catch his words. "I'm sorry."

"Don't be silly, Bill," she'd said, fighting the tears

that threatened to spill over. "The only thing that matters is you getting well. There's nothing to be sorry about. I love you."

Suddenly Bill had gripped her hand tightly with a strength that she hadn't known he still possessed. His eyes had held a wild searching look, desperate, as though all his energies were focused on his next words.

"Liz, listen to me," he'd whispered urgently, the words halting but compelling in their intensity. "I want you to do something for me. I know it will be hard." For a moment he'd stopped and closed his eyes, struggling to find the breath to continue. "I want you to help me go. This isn't life. Hooked up to machines. In pain. Liz, I know I'm dying. Help me get it over with. For me. You. The kids. It's better. I love you. Please do it for me."

Holding on to the edge of the bed, she'd had to force herself to loosen her grip on his hand. Bill's plea had reached her as though from the bottom of a deep canyon. The words had seemed to echo all around her. What was he asking her to do? She'd wanted to scream, to shake him, to make him get up out of that bed and walk away with her, a whole man. Burning tears had escaped from the corners of her eyes, squeezed tightly shut against the nightmare of this new reality. He was asking her to kill him. Slowly she'd opened her eyes and looked down at her husband. The effort of speaking had exhausted him, and he had drifted into a pained sleep. His hoarse, ragged breathing had echoed in her ears. She'd had to get away.

Sipping the scalding cafeteria coffee, Liz felt her raw, empty stomach protest against the unwelcome acidity. Automatically she took a bite of the leathery

Danish. The possibility of ever being interested in food again seemed remote indeed. She remembered the elaborately laden buffets provided by the hotel in Hawaii—how she had cracked lobster claws, extracted the meat and hand-fed Bill, following the seafood with sweet, dripping chunks of mango and papaya. It all seemed so far away! And yet it was less than a year ago. Now the same man who had brought her to shuddering ecstasy under the tropical stars was asking her to help him die.

It took Liz a while to hear her name. When she looked up from her coffee, Stuart Brooks was sitting opposite her hunched in his overcoat, his eyes dark with concern.

"Liz. The nurse said I could find you here. How are you?" He reached over and took her hand in both of his. She felt their warmth as though from a great distance, a sense of the comfort they could give . . . and of how little that comfort could help her now.

"Hello, Stuart," she managed to say. It was somehow a great effort to speak, to remember the normal everyday words that people spoke to each other. "I'm all right."

For one brief moment, she thought of spilling it all out to him. Suddenly she longed to fling herself against his chest, to lose herself in his arms. Whatever it would take to make the world just go away. But this wasn't a burden she could share with anyone. Not even Stuart Brooks, who had had his share of pain. His wife was suffering from terminal cancer; he didn't need the burden of the kind of decision she had to make. It was hers alone.

She attempted a smile and squeezed his hands in response. "I'm all right," she repeated.

Chapter Three

An Anguished Decision

Liz hadn't been able to sleep all night. Tossing and turning in bed, she'd finally gotten up and put on a flannel robe and thick socks, then stumbled wearily into the kitchen to make herself a cup of hot chocolate laced with brandy. Now she sat staring into the cold fireplace, her arms wrapped around her chest. The house wasn't cold, but she felt a core of ice deep inside her that refused to melt. Images of Bill lying alone in the hospital bed kept returning to haunt her. Was he awake? Was he frightened? How did it feel to know that he was going to die? The questions tormented her.

Could she shoulder the responsibility for taking the life of another human being? How dare Bill ask that of her? But how could she stand by and see him in such pain? The doctor had said there was no hope of his recovering. He might go on for a while on life-support machines. But it was only a matter of time.

Did she owe this to Bill? Was it morally right? Liz had never officially renounced the church, but religion had somehow drifted out of her life. When the kids were growing up she and Bill had been careful to get them to Sunday school each week; but as they'd entered adolescence, getting them to give up their friends and activities in favor of a church service had become close to impossible. Liz smiled harshly, painfully, and hugged her memories to herself as she remembered their Sunday mornings together. She and Bill had had so many wonderful Sundays since he'd come back. Breakfast and the paper in bed. Suddenly—often while they'd been in the middle of the crossword puzzle—he would take the paper from her hands and put it on the floor beside the bed.

"That's enough brain power for one morning," he would growl. "How 'bout a little of what else you got?"

Tears pricked her eyes and she felt the sobs well up inside her. She would never again share those languid, passionate, wonderfully safe Sunday mornings with Bill. Never. The word had such a final, terrifying sound.

If only she remembered how to pray. She had to find an answer somehow. It was funny how you ended up turning to God when something seemed too big to handle. Sure, she had prayed before. Kneeling in church or giving thanks before dinner. And it's not that she hadn't meant it then. But this was different. She needed an answer; she needed divine counsel. And if she couldn't talk to God, whom else could she turn to?

It wasn't fair to bring the kids in on this—not when it involved their own father. Besides, as a doctor, Snapper's medical code of ethics prohibited his involvement in something like this. She wasn't going to be responsible for ruining Snapper's career—and neither was Bill, for that matter. No. This was something she had to face without the support of the children.

Suddenly Stuart Brooks' face filled her mind. She had felt so safe this afternoon when he'd held her hands in the cafeteria. It might not be fair for her to share this with him, but if she couldn't talk to someone, she would go mad. Liz looked up at the living room clock: 11:15. Would he be at home asleep? Was he lying next to Jennifer wondering about the same things—death, loneliness? Jennifer wasn't in a hospital bed yet, but Liz knew that her cancer had progressed.

Not allowing herself to think, Liz walked to the telephone and dialed. The phone was picked up before the second ring.

"Hello?"

Liz immediately recognized Stuart's calm, deep voice. Now it held an edge of alarm with which she was more than familiar. "Stuart, it's only Liz," she replied quickly. "I'm sorry to call this late. I hope I didn't wake you." She paused, not sure how to continue. "I . . . I was just sitting here. I couldn't sleep. And I was just thinking . . . I was wondering if we could talk."

Before the words were even out, Stuart interrupted. "Is everything all right? Is it Bill?"

"Bill's the same. That's just it. There's something I have to talk to you about. I don't know who else to turn to." Once again she felt tears threatening to erupt with the leashed power of a tidal wave. She closed her eyes and pressed her fist deep into her stomach. Something about Stuart's strength, his openness and willingness to be there, made her feel so . . . vulnerable.

"I'll be right over. Hold on."

Liz cradled the receiver and covered her face with both hands. Already her burden felt lighter.

It seemed almost impossible, but two hours later Liz found herself laughing. Stuart had arrived at the front door and knocked softly. It was obvious he had dressed in a hurry, but Liz was nevertheless struck by how ruggedly handsome he was. His smooth silver hair was slightly rumpled. He had pulled on an old ski sweater and jeans, and he looked so alive and vital that for a moment Liz felt weak.

"Thank you for coming, Stuart," she said. And then burst into tears.

Looking back on it, she couldn't tell if she had cried for ten minutes or two hours. She sat in an armchair, curled into herself, her hair damp with tears, the sobs finally subsiding. Stuart sat across from her, watching. It was as though he sensed her need to be alone, and yet not alone. She was locked in her own private hell, but somehow having him there made her feel that she would not get lost, that she would emerge on the other side.

Finally she sat up and accepted the handkerchief Stuart offered. She blew her nose long and hard and took a deep, shuddering breath.

"Bill has asked me to help him die."

There was a long silence. Liz could feel herself holding her breath.

"You know, I've often wondered what I would do if Jennifer asked me to do the same thing." Stuart gazed deep into the rug, far away in his thoughts.

"And what did you decide?"

"I didn't. I think it's something that you can't understand or know about until it happens. And it's happened to you."

He looked up and stared directly into her eyes. Liz

felt her lips tremble again, and she struggled for control.

"But I'm scared. I don't know how I feel. I feel angry at him for making me do this. But I can't stand to see his pain. What if that was me lying there, or one of my children, begging to end the pain? How can I possibly refuse him?"

Suddenly Stuart was kneeling on the floor in front of her chair. She felt his strong hands grip her arms. The lamplight reflected off the silver in his hair, making it gleam.

"Liz, you're strong enough to do this," he said, his blue eyes gazing deeply into hers. "You want to end Bill's suffering. That's all that counts."

Before she knew what happened, she was on the floor and in his arms. He held her, rocking her, murmuring soothing, unintelligible words, smoothing back her hair. Part of her felt like a child being rocked to sleep; part of her was responding to Stuart as a woman. She could feel the muscles in his arm tensing against her breast, his gentle, steady breathing on her hair. Closing her eyes, she breathed in the warm, smoky scent of his wool sweater. It reminded her of Bill. How good it felt to be in a man's arms again! She wished she could stay there forever.

Later, Stuart tucked her into bed and stayed with her until she became drowsy. Before her eyes closed, she noticed by the hands of her bedside clock that it was 2:15. A protest rose to her lips: she had kept him so long.

"Thank you, Stuart. You're a good friend," she murmured, her eyes and voice heavy with exhaustion.

"I'll always be here if you need me."

They were the last words she heard before falling into a heavy, dreamless sleep.

Kay Chancellor hung up the phone feeling triumphant. It was the third time in a week that Jack Curtis had called asking to speak to Joanna, and this time she hadn't pulled any punches.

"Why do you want to talk to her?"

"What do you mean, *why?*" he'd asked, fury lacing his voice. "She's my ex-wife. And besides, it's none of your business why I want to talk to her."

"Well, she doesn't want to talk to you." Kay hadn't tried to hide the triumph in her voice. "She specifically told me that if you called, I was supposed to say she wasn't in. In fact, if you want the direct quote, she said, 'Tell that conceited bastard that I never want to speak to him again as long as I live.'"

Kay found the lie had slipped easily off her tongue. In actual fact, nothing was farther from the truth. She found it increasingly annoying that Joanna couldn't seem to stop talking about Jack Curtis. She felt as though she had listened to every intimate detail there was to hear about their ridiculous marriage. She couldn't understand why Joanna was so attached to the guy, particularly after he'd dropped her the way he did. He had gone and married another woman, and she was still making excuses for him.

"Well, Kay, I really was fat. I mean real fat," Joanna replied when Kay asked her. "There's nothing that Jack hates more than fat." She sighed, then complacently smoothed the brand-new pink satin teddy that Kay had bought her the day before. "Sometimes I wonder if that's why I got so fat." She giggled and brightened. "Do you think that's why?"

Kay walked up behind Joanna where she had sat down at her dressing table to brush her hair. Taking the brush from Joanna's hand, she began to do the job herself with long, lingering strokes, watching her protegée in the mirror.

"I don't think you're too fat at all, honey. And I don't know what's wrong with these men, anyway. They seem to want skin and bones. What's wrong with a little padding? But the way you were eating those snails yesterday, we're going to have to watch out for that waistline." Playfully she spanked Joanna on her hip with the hairbrush.

"Oh, Kay, you're so good to me." Joanna turned to hug the older woman with a sudden rush of feeling. She had to admit that lately Kay had been acting a little bit more like a prison warden than a roommate. Once, when she'd wanted to meet a friend for dinner and asked Kay if she could borrow the car, she'd gotten a thirty-minute inquisition. In the end it had been easier to call up her friend with an excuse and spend the evening with Kay.

It wasn't that she didn't like Kay. Maybe she even loved her. Kay was the most generous person she had ever known. But now that she had grown used to all the clothes and the gifts, the flowers and the lessons about wineglasses and fish forks, she was beginning to feel a little antsy. What she wouldn't give to sneak out one night and go dancing! Have a bunch of beers and really let loose. She felt like she was always pretending with Kay, trying to think of what would please her—never doing and saying what she really felt.

And then two nights ago in the middle of the night, Kay had come into her room. Joanna had pretended to be asleep. Kay had roamed around the bedroom, quietly picking up her hairbrush and putting it down again, stroking the heavy silk of her Japanese kimono, another gift. Then Joanna had heard her move over to the bed and stand next to it. She'd tried to keep her breathing even, to keep her eyelids from fluttering. What was the woman doing? She had reached out and oh, so gently pushed a stray hair back in place. It was a comforting gesture, almost like a mother's—but not quite. It had made Joanna feel uncomfortable. Kay was getting too close, stepping over a few too many boundaries. Didn't she have a right to some privacy?

Maybe it was time to start thinking about moving out.

Jill Foster found that her daily trips to the hospital to visit her father were now tinged with a feeling of anticipation. *Today, I'm going to see David again*, she would think every morning. Since the day she had entered David Mallory's hospital room by mistake, she had spent hours at his bedside, talking and laughing, reading to him from books and magazines or just sitting quietly, watching him.

He already knew practically everything there was to know about her. She found that things just spilled out from her around him. With just a word or two, he could coax things out of her, feelings and memories, stories of her childhood that had been bottled up for years. It was strange, though. She really didn't know much about him. Each time she tried to turn the conversation and ask about his life, he somehow managed to avoid answering her. She did know that he was an engineering contractor, and that he had sustained an accident on a work site in Genoa City that had caused the gradual deterioration of his vision.

He also seemed to have few visitors. Once when she had arrived to visit, Jill saw a beautiful blond woman leaving his room. The stab of jealousy she felt was clear and sharp. When she questioned David about the woman, he simply said that she was "just a friend." Jill had felt it would be ridiculous to pry further. But she hadn't been able to put the lovely woman out of her mind.

Today she had dressed carefully, wearing a new soft wool jersey dress that hugged her figure, daubing a special new perfume behind her ears and on her wrists and painstakingly applying makeup. She wanted to look her best, just as if David could really see her. Today was the day she would tell him how she was going to help him see again.

She pushed open the door and tiptoed into the room, not wanting to awaken him. His slow smile told her he was already up.

"I have the feeling that a mighty pretty rose just walked into my room," he drawled. "Come over here and let me smell you."

The next minute he had pulled her down onto the bed so that she was lying next to him.

"David!" she protested. "Someone might come in!"

"I've wanted to do this since the first day you walked in here," David murmured into her ear. His arm tightened around her as he pressed her to his chest. She could feel his heart pounding under the thin cloth of his hospital gown. The heat emanating from his chest was incredible. She felt her own heart race in time with his.

Gently he turned her face toward his and sought her lips. Jill's body melted as his lips explored hers, tasting, savoring. Her head swam, lost in a swirl of longing. She raised her hand to caress his face, his hair, and she suddenly felt the bandages. She opened her eyes. What were they doing? She felt the heat in her face. Her lips felt full and red with longing.

"David," she said, her voice catching with stifled desire. She moved to a sitting position on the bed and hastily straightened her blouse. "We shouldn't be doing this."

"Why not?" He laughed softly, reaching for her again. "I said I was going blind, not senseless." He reached for her again, but Jill scrambled off the bed and smoothed back her hair.

"David," she said, taking his hand. "I have something wonderful to tell you. Well, part of it is wonderful. Your part." She hesitated, afraid to continue. "Daddy has left all of his organs to the hospital. I thought I remembered Mom saying so, but I asked the nurse to look it up in his hospital records, and it's true. David, that means his eyes."

David suddenly grew serious, his voice tight. "But your father is alive."

"I know," Jill said. She heard the defensive tone in her voice and hurried on. "We all know he's going to die. It's just a matter of time. And when he does, you can have his eyes!" she finished triumphantly. David continued to frown. "Well, you do want to see again, don't you?" she asked sarcastically, angry that David could make her feel so callous and cold. Of course she didn't want her father to die; it wasn't that. But the man hooked up to all those tubes and machines sometimes didn't even seem like her father anymore.

Anyway, wouldn't he want it that way? To give his eyes to someone who needed them . . . to a man that his own daughter . . . was in love with?

Jill was shocked at the thought that she had not yet said out loud. Love. Could she really have fallen in love with David Mallory so soon? A man she had never seen outside of a hospital room? A man who knew nothing of what his future might hold? A man whose eyes she had never looked into?

It seemed cold in Bill's room. Liz stood at his bedside clutching her coat around her. She knew that if one of the night nurses walked in, she'd be in trouble. They had bent over backward to stretch the rules and let her stay with Bill as much as possible in the last months. But being in the intensive care unit at midnight was strictly forbidden.

Liz took Bill's hand in her own and stroked it gently, rhythmically. It felt cool and already almost lifeless. The strong dark hairs that had once sprung crisply from his arms had nearly disappeared. Everything about Bill seemed smaller, wasted. She bent and placed a long silent kiss on his forehead, both cheeks and then his lips. She smoothed his hair back from his brow and gazed down at him.

"I've been thinking a lot, Bill, and praying," she whispered to his sleeping form. "And I don't know if what I'm going to do is the right thing. In the eyes of the world. Or the eyes of God. But I know it's what you want. And that's the only thing that matters." Tears streamed unnoticed down her face. A few salty drops fell on Bill's hand where it lay entwined with hers on the bed.

What she wouldn't do to be able to turn back the clock, to return to the early days of their marriage when it had seemed as though nothing could ever go wrong. Suddenly Liz remembered their first honeymoon trip to San Francisco. She remembered the tiny cove they had found where the surf came crashing in and the crisp California air whipped their hair and stung their faces with the tang of salt. They had found a place on the beach where the jutting rocks formed a tiny private bedroom covered in soft white sand. They'd made love on the beach on a bright cotton beach blanket borrowed from their hotel. The smell of the sand and the sun and the salt air seemed to fill her nostrils now; Bill's skin had been so warm and smooth, burnished by the sun, smelling faintly of clean male sweat and suntan lotion. She could remember burying her face in his shoulder, in the warm hollow of his shoulder. Gulls cawed and laughed overhead, and in the distance came the sound of muffled voices, belonging to another world. Her world was Bill, only Bill.

She could still remember so vividly the words he had said that day, as he'd wrapped them together tightly in the blanket, brushing away the tears of happiness that had coursed down her face. "We'll be together always, Liz," he'd whispered into her salt-streaked hair. "That I promise you."

Liz remembered how the words had filled her —with a sense of peace, of intense passionate belonging, of overpowering joy. She had brought Bill's dark head down to cradle it on her chest. "Forever, darling. It's not long enough. It's not long enough."

Now it was over. Bill's support machines seemed to whisper and breathe with a life of their own. Liz felt as though she were no longer inside her own skin: she seemed to be floating in a cool mist, looking down at her husband's body as though from a great distance. She heard a roaring in her ears as she reached out one hand, slowly, inexorably. "Goodbye, Bill," she whispered. "I love you."

The sudden silence filled the room. Liz took one step backward, then another, almost staggering. Her face was ashen, distant. She turned toward the door as though to leave, but one hand still reached out toward the bed where Bill lay, his chest still.

"Bill . . ." The word came out in a harsh, tortured whisper. She lurched back toward the bed, then crumpled to the floor.

Chapter Four

To Protect the Innocent

Snapper Foster had had better evenings. One of his heart patients, a young girl, had died during emergency surgery, and he had to tell the waiting family, still hoping against hope. That job was never easy, no matter what the circumstances, but it was the young ones that really got to him. It sometimes wasn't fair what nature doled out. Somewhere under the laws of compensation, this little girl had possessed one of the sweetest, brightest, sunniest and most uncomplaining dispositions ever to be handed out. And now she was gone, a whole life wasted. It just didn't seem fair.

Things could be going better at home, too. God knows, Chris was used to being a doctor's wife and the last-minute emergencies that always came up, but some things still hurt. Tonight was their anniversary, and she had planned a really special evening. But just as he'd uncorked a bottle of Dom Pérignon and they'd started to dig into a fireside feast of black caviar, smoked oysters and Chris's elegant homemade phyllo pastries filled with prosciutto, rosemary and cheese, the call had come in to go to surgery.

Now it looked as if he wasn't going to get home at all tonight.

And then of course there was the worry about his mother. Snapper knew his father was dying; as a doctor, he knew that was inevitable. He had already gone through his private mourning and was ready to face what was going to happen. It was his mother he worried about. She seemed so cold and strong, driven by some inner vision, haunted by a strange kind of guilt, as though by pushing herself to the limits of her endurance, she could pay for her husband's death . . . perhaps even replace his life with her own.

Snapper figured it would be easy enough to drop in on his father before he saw the patient in 6D. This one was a chronic complainer, a recuperating tumor case whose biggest problem was inside his own head. Attention wasn't the word for what this guy wanted. But he was also a big donor to Genoa General, and everyone treated him like an Arab sheik. So what if the guy had practically paid for the wing he was lying in? It didn't give him the right to have every damn doctor in the hospital at his beck and call.

When he reached his father's room he pushed open the door, which was standing ajar. Even before the door was fully open, the unaccustomed silence told him something was wrong. Snapper felt a wave of sadness wash over him. One look at his father lying white and still on the bed was all he needed. But he couldn't help his father now. It was his mother he rushed to. He stooped at her side and gently picked up one limp wrist. Her pulse was light and erratic, her breathing shallow. Within minutes a crew of night nurses and orderlies had rushed her to an examining room.

His father's death would be hard enough on the family; it would be far worse if anything happened to his mother. As he automatically checked her vital signs, Snapper found his thoughts returning to the scene he had walked in on. He couldn't escape the obvious conclusion. What else had his mother been doing in his father's room so late at night? He felt a sudden swell of tenderness for her. She was a brave lady to be able to do that. As a doctor he had experienced other such situations, and he'd found that most people couldn't handle the emotional pressure of helping to terminate the life of a loved one. It was the surest test of love he knew of, to be able to commit that final irrevocable act for another human being—even if it meant never again seeing someone you loved more than anyone else in the world.

But there would have to be an investigation. Somehow he was going to have to protect his mother. She had been through far too much already without having to face the burden of a trial. And it might come down to that. To anyone with a brain and a heart, what she had done was simply the act of a thinking, feeling human being. But to a lot of other people, that simple act of humanity was called something else.

It was called murder.

Jill felt numb. The night before, Snapper had called her with the news while she was in bed asleep. Now she sat in the hospital waiting room sipping a cold cup of coffee, trying to sort out her feelings.

She had known her father was going to die, but somehow she had never quite believed that it could really happen. She had lost her father for all those years when he had left Genoa City—and now she had

53

lost him forever. Just thinking about all that lost time filled her with impotent rage. He would never see his grandchildren grow up. She would never again know the comfort of having her father there, patient, loving, sympathetic, always there to listen when she was troubled or had a problem. He was simply gone.

And now there was her mother to worry about. They were still waiting for the tests that would show what had happened. Snapper was convinced that her collapse had been caused by a stroke brought on by the shock of Bill's death. Jill wasn't altogether satisfied with Snapper's answers to her questions. He seemed evasive, as though he knew a lot more than he was telling her. But Jill hadn't wanted to press him too hard.

The one thing that had helped her endure all this was David. When she'd arrived at the hospital that morning, before seeing Snapper or even her mother, she had walked into David's room. He'd looked up, cocking his head in the familiar way that made his eyebrows seem raised inquiringly, even though they were hidden behind bandages. It was almost as if he could feel her pain.

"Jill?" he'd asked gently, his arm outstretched. She'd run to him and fallen across his chest, shaken by sobs.

"Daddy's dead," was all she'd been able to say.

David had stroked her hair, murmuring soft, consoling sounds. "It's all right, darling. I know. Snapper told me. He's not in pain anymore. He's at peace now. He can rest. Shhh." The soothing motion of his hand had quieted her sobs until at last she was still.

David's heart had pounded slowly and steadily under hers, filling her for the moment with a welcome sense of peace. It seemed so ironic that she had

really met David through her father. If her father
hadn't been sick and dying, lying in the intensive
care unit of Genoa General, they would probably
never have met.

Fate was a strange thing, she mused now as she sat
in the waiting room. Maybe that ancient wisdom was
true—the Lord giveth and the Lord taketh away. She
would give anything to bring her father back, but
losing him was so much easier to bear knowing that
David was at her side. It was funny; she had barely
had a chance to see David outside of his hospital
room, and yet for her he was a pillar of strength. She
wondered if she could be so supportive if the situation were reversed. He had done so much for her
already, and now it was time to do something for
him.

Jill pressed her lips firmly together and nodded her
head once, her decision made. Snapper had a lot on
his mind right now, but time was really crucial here.
She wanted David to have his operation—which
meant he had to have her father's cornea. She
thought her father would have wanted it that way.
She didn't care what other people thought. David
was alive, very much alive, and in desperate need.
Daddy wasn't the kind of person who would have
stood around at such times worrying about propriety
—what people thought. He was a doer, someone
who stood up in a crowd and spoke his mind. Well,
she was his daughter. And she was about to show
everyone what a Foster was made of.

Liz seemed to float back to the world from a great
distance. Her head felt foggy, misshapen, and there
was a dull throbbing in the back of her head. Where
was she, anyway? And how was Bill? Her thoughts

came disjointed, confused. She struggled to sit up but found herself too weak to do so. When she looked down the length of her arm, she saw that she was hooked up to IV equipment. What had happened to her? She had to find out about Bill, she fretted. He could be in pain or waking up to find himself alone. She had to be with him. Once more she struggled in vain to rise to a sitting position. The effort exhausted her. Just for a minute, then—she would lie back down and think for just a minute. Her head fell back heavily into the pillow and she slept.

"Snapper, you know I hate to do this to you." Dr. Bendicks stood looking out of his office window at the bleak winter landscape, his hands thrust deep into the pockets of his slacks. "You know you're like a son to me." He turned and looked intently at Snapper, who sat in a chair opposite a large office desk strewn with papers. "But, hell, I have no choice. This case has to go before the committee, and until it does I can't have you practicing medicine in my hospital. You're a damn good doctor, one of the best Genoa General has ever had. I know that. But as long as suspicion of your father's death is focused upon you, I'm going to have to put you on suspension and have you turn your case load over to another doctor. I don't have to tell you how much it hurts me to do this, Snapper. Hopefully this whole thing will be cleared up before long. But since you're refusing to let your mother be implicated in your father's death, the finger points right at you. I know the state your mother's in; I know you don't want to cause her any more pain. But you have your career to think of, your wife. Won't you reconsider?"

"No," Snapper said dully. He slumped low in the comfortable leather armchair, remembering how many times he had sat in the same chair and received wise counsel from this man—his mentor, his friend. Dr. Bendicks had helped him through medical school, played father to him when he needed one and his own hadn't been around. Sometimes Snapper felt that Frank Bendicks was more a father to him than his own. They had a kind of closeness that he and his real father had never managed to achieve. Maybe it was just because Dr. Bendicks *wasn't* his father that they could get so close. When he'd had problems in his marriage, it was Frank Bendicks he had turned to for counsel, not his father.

But this time he couldn't follow his advice, no matter how wise. The tests had proved he was right; his mother had suffered a mild stroke. She had sustained virtually no paralysis, however, and the prognosis for a full recovery was good. The problem was she couldn't remember what she had done. As far as she was concerned, her husband was still alive. Not only did she not know that he was gone, she seemed to have no awareness that she herself had liberated him from the life he could no longer endure.

Snapper sat hunched at the edge of his armchair, his hands clenched at his side. Suddenly he brought them down on top of the desk. "Frank, I have no choice! I can't have my mother go through a trial. God knows what it could do to her. Her mental state is too fragile—a shock like this could send her right over the edge. What else can I do? I'm hoping that they can prove natural causes and that my name will be cleared. You know the man was ready to go any day—any minute, for that matter. Mom just couldn't stand by and see him in pain; I don't blame her. If I weren't a doctor here, I would probably have done it myself."

Snapper stood up and paced the office. When he reached the far wall near the door, he stopped and pounded his fist against the wall. "*Damn* it! I'm a good doctor, and I've seen my share of unethical practice, you and I both have. If they throw the book at me for this, I'm not going to have a lot of respect for my own profession. I can prove I didn't do it. I have witnesses that will testify I couldn't have. But I don't want the blame to fall on my mother. She's just undergone the biggest shock in her life. And I'm not going to have this on my conscience."

Dr. Bendicks walked up behind Snapper and put one hand on his shoulder. Slowly Snapper turned around, and they looked hard into each other's eyes. "I'm sorry about your father, son," he said, and pulled him into his arms in a long, hard embrace.

Greg Foster had provided legal counsel before in cases of mercy killings. But this one was a little different—this case concerned the death of his own father. For a moment he felt tears threaten, and his throat closed painfully. *Stop it!* he commanded himself. *You aren't going to be able to help Snapper if you lose control.* He knew he had to think clearly and precisely during the inquest and not let his own emotions interfere with his position as his brother's attorney.

God, his own big brother, the doctor. How ironic life is, he mused. He remembered how he had idolized Snapper growing up. Snapper, who had always seemed so sure of himself, sure of his path in life, while he had always seemed to stumble along in big brother's shadow, never quite good enough, always second best. Snapper had helped put him through law school while he was doing his residency, working two jobs, living on two, sometimes three hours of sleep a night.

And then there was Chris. For as long as he could remember, Snapper's beautiful wife was the only woman that Greg could ever imagine loving. It had angered him when Snapper would go off and leave Chris alone for days on end, even though he knew that the hours away weren't Snapper's fault or his choice. He would fantasize about going over to the apartment and taking Snapper's place, confessing his love to Chris, carrying her into the bedroom . . .

Guilt at his own thoughts made his anger for Snapper turn inside, against himself. The years had smoothed things out, paved the way for a new relationship as brothers. But still the antagonism lay dormant. Greg tried to find it now, find the source of that festering sore he kept inside him. What did he feel about his brother? If Snapper had killed their father, could he blame him? Greg was sure they had all thought about it at one point or another. He certainly had after his last visit to his father. Seeing him lying in bed, gaunt, ashen, practically unrecognizable. Was he just angry and jealous because Snapper had once again stolen the limelight? Because somehow or other Snapper was going to walk away the hero one more time.

Angrily, Greg pushed aside the bitter thoughts and sorted the stack of papers in front of him. Perhaps he could get the charges dropped, he thought. One of the night nurses had been with Snapper at the estimated time of death. She was going to show up for the hearing. Greg would then declare his mother unfit to testify, pending further notice. The case would get put on permanent hold, and Snapper could resume his case load, record cleared. Their mother could deal with recuperating, and the pain of remembering, at her own pace . . . when her mind told her she was strong enough to know the truth.

Greg closed his briefcase firmly. There was only one thing he needed to know before he defended Snapper in front of the hospital board. It would have no bearing on how he tried the case; it was for himself alone. He needed to know if Snapper had been there and watched while his mother had ended their father's life.

Joanna looked at the pile of clothes she had accumulated on the bed and turned back to the mirror with a sigh. Clothes seemed to be such a big deal these days. Sure, she loved all the new things Kay had given her. But lately all the generosity seemed more like a burden than anything else. Joanna would never have believed it of herself just a few short months ago, but sometimes she longed for the days when she used to throw her folded carpenter's apron into her knapsack, put on her blue-jean skirt and a cotton turtleneck and head off for her waitressing shift. All this pampering was getting on her nerves. But maybe it was good to get it out of her system.

Ever since she could remember, she had been envious of the ladies she saw through store windows as she passed by—pampered, elegantly dressed women getting manicures and pedicures and waiting to be given massages or facials as though they didn't have a care in the world. She would be walking by doing mental calculations, trying to figure out how to squeeze the food shopping out of the budget for that week, and the sight of all that luxury made her want to scream. She knew it was childish, but it just didn't seem fair. Those women showed how rich and spoiled they were through every well-creamed pore in their bodies. Exhausted, Joanna would dream of being whisked off to a spa in the south of France by a wonderfully handsome, wealthy gentleman.

Not that being with Kay was the least bit like being with a handsome, sexy, rich man. Not by a long shot. For starters, Joanna was beginning to wonder if Kay wasn't just a little bit too interested in her. Somehow she always seemed to be around when Joanna was getting dressed or undressed, or about to take a shower. She had an almost proprietary air about her, as though putting some fancy threads on Joanna's back gave her a right to survey the merchandise whenever she damn well pleased. Well, she had another think coming.

Joanna pinned a new *faux* diamond brooch to the lapel of her Perry Ellis suit and stepped back to survey the effect. Yes, she was looking pretty good these days. Too bad Jack wasn't around to see. He always thought women in tailored suits and high heels were a million times more sexy than they were in frills and flounces. And he'd have gone crazy over this one, she thought with a satisfied little smirk.

But oh, God, how she missed him, she realized, suddenly sober. Was he happy in his new marriage with Peggy? she wondered. Peggy had always seemed too delicate for Jack. Or maybe she was just jealous. Peggy was a sweet woman, she had to admit. They had even been friends for a while, Peggy taking her under her wing and showing her what a real friend was all about. And then shafting her royally, she thought bitterly. Stealing Jack right out from under her nose, and then acting hurt because Joanna didn't feel right being friends anymore . . . didn't exactly trust her.

Why did she seem to spend her life falling into the clutches of scheming women? And what on earth was she going to do about Kay? The scene in the restaurant the other day had really been the last straw.

Joanna had met Jake, an old friend of hers and Jack's, for lunch. They'd been enjoying a glass of wine before their salads arrived, reminiscing and catching up, when Joanna had seen Kay storm out of her car and into the restaurant. . . .

"Oh, no," she whispered under her breath, cupping her hand over her forehead as if to protect herself from Kay's lashing fury.

"What the hell do you think you're doing going off without telling me!" she screeched. Jake's eyes widened with surprise, and he made a gesture toward Joanna as though to ask whether she wanted him to intervene.

"Kay, this is Jake," Joanna said coldly. "What on earth are you talking about? I'm just meeting an old friend for lunch, as you can see," she added with exaggerated sarcasm. "I don't have to get your permission every time I breathe. I'm a grown woman, and I'll thank you to treat me like one." She turned back to the table and took a gulp of her Chardonnay. She could feel the high spots of color in her cheeks. How dare that old witch embarrass her in front of the entire restaurant? Was she totally out of her mind? For a moment Joanna felt a stab of real fear. She knew that Kay Chancellor had a history of problems, drinking and otherwise. But then, who didn't? Yet what about all that roaming around she did at night, and her jealous, possessive fury? Maybe the lady was a little around the bend.

For the hundredth time, as she kissed Jake good-bye and backed Kay's Mercedes out of the parking lot, she wondered what she was doing. Moving into traffic, she realized she wasn't ready yet to drive back to the Chancellor home. She had to get some air first, to breathe and feel like herself again—whatever that was. Lately, she had been dreaming about Jack even more often. Practically every morning she woke up, sometimes crying, sometimes laughing. Jack was a decent man, even if he had dumped her. She'd never met anyone who could make everything in the world seem so fascinating. Jack just had that ability. And he had plenty of others, too. It seemed like an eternity since they'd been to bed together, even though it was really only a few months. So much had happened in those months. She looked down at her sleek calves and thighs in their sheer slate stockings. Yes, a lot had happened in those months.

Without realizing it, almost as though the car had a mind of its own, she found herself driving down the block near their old home. Peggy's home now, she thought angrily. It had hurt her that Jack had wanted to bring his new bride back to the same house where they had been so happy together in the beginning. It seemed almost sacrilegious, as though he were violating or dismissing those years by not cherishing their memory—by his willingness to replace those memories with new ones of Peggy.

But what did it all really matter? she thought wearily as she drove slowly by the house. Jack wasn't her husband anymore. He loved another woman. And what they did in the privacy of their own home was something she really didn't want to know anything about. . . .

* * *

Inside his house, Jack Curtis was carelessly sticking a dozen red roses in an old quart juice jar he'd found in the trash. That was where they really belonged, anyway, he thought, along with his marriage.

Ever since the honeymoon, when they had returned to Genoa City, Jack had been waiting. He thought Peggy would leave him and go home immediately, but she had stayed, almost as though to prove something to herself. Night after night, Jack had come home with little gifts—records, flowers, bottles of champagne, trinkets—determined to coax Peggy closer to him. All he wanted to do was be able to talk to her—really talk, not these stiff, formal little conversations they conducted about the weather, his day at the office, and when the shirts would be ready at the cleaners. He couldn't stand too much more. He found himself snapping at his secretary at the college and glowering at his students when they came to see him during office hours. Something had to give soon or he would go crazy.

His initial feelings of guilt about calling his ex-wife had been replaced by anger at the realization that she was as unavailable to him as if she were living under armed guard. Joanna had always been so *available*, like a happy, welcoming puppy whenever he'd wanted her. Maybe that was one of the reasons their marriage hadn't worked: he'd taken her for granted, looked down on her somehow, and that had demoralized her into a pattern of abusive eating. He felt guilty about that. Really guilty.

He was a smart guy, and he knew enough about psychology to realize that eating disorders stemmed from some deep-rooted unhappiness. He had sat there watching Joanna blow up like a blimp, so wrapped up in himself, in his own self-image and how her weight made *him* look, that he hadn't even bothered to help her. Once in a while he had asked if she wanted to talk. But not once had he really *helped* her, in a way that was unselfish and counted for something. He simply hadn't been there for her.

Was that why he couldn't get her out of his mind now? His marriage to Peggy was such a disappointment—no, forget disappointment. A disaster. And he was feeling guilty all over again. Why was he always fatally attracted to women with such terrible problems?

He'd come in tonight with a dozen roses, a bottle of champagne and a silly grin on his face, as though any of that were going to make a difference. It was like trying to patch the cracks in a burst dam.

And then he'd tried to kiss her. She was standing woodenly in front of the kitchen sink peeling carrots, and he'd slipped up behind her, put his arm around her waist and kissed her cheek. She'd stiffened, and he could feel her body begin to tremble.

"Come on, Peggy honey," he'd coaxed, "try to relax." From over her shoulder he'd caught sight of her hand where it rested on the edge of the sink. He'd watched, strangely fascinated, his own body stiffening, as her knuckles had tightened and turned white on the handle of the knife she held clenched in her right hand.

Liz stared into the white light that shone in her eyes, squinting as it seemed to pierce her brain. Why did they keep doing that to her? And where was Bill? She needed to remind him to take his chest medicine. He always forgot, and she was the only one he would listen to. Where was he? she thought, clutching at the hospital blanket, hardly seeing the two doctors, one of them her son, who stood at the foot of her bed studying her chart.

Chapter Five

A Change of Heart

Stuart Brooks had lost track of the number of times he'd been into the florist at Genoa General in the last week. The bouquets of fresh flowers were all beginning to look the same to him. He'd bought Jennifer roses twice, irises once and last time a potted begonia. Other people had been sending flowers, and the room had become cloying with the mixed scents. One of the first things he did when he went to her room this time, after kissing her thin cheek, was to check all the flowers, discarding the ones that had died and freshening the water in the vases of those that could last another day or two. Somehow the activity made him feel less helpless, as though by taking care of her flowers he could somehow bring his wife back to her old self.

Jennifer had endured bravely for a long time, but finally even she couldn't go on at home anymore, hiding her pain from him and from the children. It hadn't come as a surprise. They'd all been waiting, acting cheerful and keeping up the activity of a normal, bustling household. But the knowledge had been there: sooner or later her cancer was going to win.

Peggy, as usual, was the hardest hit when her mother returned to the hospital, with the knowledge heavy in the air that this time was probably going to be the last. Stuart was worried about Peggy. They'd had their ups and downs, like most fathers and daughters, their share of fights and disagreements. But he loved her and felt a special closeness toward her. His other daughters had never seemed to need him as much; they always seemed to be running ahead with their lives faster than he could keep up. But Peggy was different; she had a certain gentleness, a frailty about her, that made her road in life a difficult one. And he couldn't say that he approved of her marriage. In fact, it worried the hell out of him. He remembered the ugly argument they'd had when he found out she was still seeing Jack Curtis. He didn't approve of a woman going out with a married man—and he never would. Maybe he was old-fashioned, but he figured you couldn't trust a man who felt comfortable cheating on his own wife, no matter what the circumstances. If a marriage wasn't working, you got out of it.

Peggy had seemed happy enough right before the wedding, but the last time he'd called her she had sounded so young and alone, her voice barely loud enough for him to hear or understand her. She'd insisted everything was fine, but he just didn't believe her. And she'd been so upset when he'd suggested coming by for a visit. What was she hiding? They had only been back from their weekend honeymoon for a few weeks. Could something be so terribly wrong so early in the marriage?

Jennifer had tried hard to calm his fears. Peggy was a grown woman, she'd argued, able to make her own choices. Besides, you couldn't make choices for anyone else.

He had always loved Jennifer's sane, unruffled approach to life. Where he was usually ready to fly off the handle or jump to conclusions, Jennifer was as steady as a rock, ever the cool, calm voice of reason. More often than not he and his wife would end up laughing together at his temper or his impatience.

Stuart never ceased to marvel at how brave she was. Even now she smiled at him and held out her hand as he came into the room. "Hello, darling," she said, her voice husky with emotion and tinged with pain.

He held her close, feeling with a heart-wrenching pang how thin she had become. Their conversations were usually brief; Jennifer asked about one of the girls, or how Stuart was coping at the newspaper or with problems around the house. They both did their best to keep the conversation light. Mostly they talked to each other with their eyes, gazing deeply at one another in the way of people who have loved a long time. There were no secrets left anymore. All feelings of betrayal or bitterness were gone, replaced only with an enormous sadness. They had so much. They were losing so much.

Stuart had hardly ever cried in his life. Once or twice when he was a young boy, he could remember crying. But even back then tears had come to him only with great difficulty. And now, when he left the hospital after visiting hours and sat in his car, he would rest his head against the steering wheel and try to cry out the wrenching pain of his loss. He was going to lose Jennifer. He knew that, and yet it was so hard to accept.

After picking out half a dozen yellow roses for his wife, he selected a lush potted African violet. He would go in and see Liz for a while tonight. Stuart often thought of Liz Foster, of how much he felt for what she had to endure . . . was still enduring. He knew from Snapper that Liz still hadn't recovered from her stroke enough to remember that her husband was dead. Twice now, Stuart had gone into her room and stood by her bedside, looking down at her sleeping form, and then left quietly. Tonight, after Jennifer fell asleep, Stuart left his wife's room, his grip so tight on the African violet that he thought his hand might crush it. Underneath his numbness, he felt an uncontrollable anger. His wife was leaving him. He had nothing to say in the matter, no control. All he could do was buy her flowers and tell her he loved her. Against what she suffered, it was nothing. She still moved relentlessly away, slipping further and further from his grasp.

There was a small light on in Liz's room next to her bed. Her face looked more peaceful tonight, less disturbed in its sleep, he thought as he stared down at her. Pulling up a chair next to her bed, Stuart sat down and took her hand. Suddenly, he broke. His shoulders heaved, and he felt the tears come. They scalded his cheeks, as though the weeks and months of fear and waiting had brought them to the boiling point. And even as they spilled over, he felt a sense of release.

Then, through his grief, he felt Liz's hand soothing his. He looked up and saw that her eyes were open. She didn't say anything, but their eyes met in wordless sympathy, as though the depth of his pain had reached her in a way nothing else could. For a moment her eyes seemed to lose the dazed, faraway look that had haunted them for the past week. She was Liz again. Stuart gripped her hand and pressed his lips to her gently curled fingers, welcoming her back.

When he looked up, she was asleep.

Greg hadn't felt so comfortable around his brother in years.

"Well, I have to say for a kid brother you did a really great job," Snapper said, leaning over to touch Greg's shoulder. "Seriously, thanks, Greg. That could have been my career in a sling if you hadn't been able to come through for me. But I knew you'd do it. I have faith, little brother."

Was it really that simple? Greg wondered to himself. Was it all just a matter of proving that he was good enough? He remembered how when they were kids, Snapper had always been the athletic one, the popular one. In high school, Snapper was captain of the football team as well as valedictorian—not to mention the fact that he was dating the most beautiful girl in the school. Greg had spent his time with the debating club and his law books, not even bothering to compete. His was such a classic case of sibling jealousy that it was almost embarrassing. But textbook or not, it certainly had taken him long enough to get over the feelings of competitiveness and animosity.

Now here he was, all these years later, finally feeling as if he were on an equal footing with his big brother. And look what it had taken to get him to feel like that—his father's dying and his brother being wrongly accused of his death.

The inquest had gone just as Greg had predicted it would. The night nurse had made a perfect witness, calm, intelligent, and wholly believable. Once Snapper's whereabouts at the time of death had been substantiated, it was a simple enough matter to tie up the case and leave it pending the future health of the deceased's wife. Their mother. Snapper had slapped him on the back and invited him out for a beer to celebrate.

They sat in a booth at a tavern near the hospital, clinked their frosty glasses of draft beer, then raised them to their lips and drank.

Greg slowly twisted his mug around and around, making interlocking wet rings on the checkered tablecloth. Suddenly he looked directly at Snapper. "I hope you didn't mind my asking you that question before the inquest. I just couldn't go ahead until I knew. Do you understand?"

"Yeah, I think so. I figure you needed to know exactly what happened. Deserved to know. You're sticking your neck out for me, and that's the least I can do. I hope you believe me. But I can't honestly say that if I'd walked in on Mom, I'd have stopped her. That's something I'll never really know." He paused, then raised his glass to take a long gulp of his ale. "What about you? What would you have done?"

There was a long silence while Greg folded and unfolded his napkin. "I don't know. It would be easy for me to say that I wouldn't let Mom go through with something like that. That I would have felt the need to save Dad. I suppose I can't help but wonder how much longer he would have lived. I know it didn't look good, but there are such things as total remissions. There are cases that seem hopeless and then suddenly turn around at the last minute. Isn't that true, Snapper? You're the doctor."

Snapper looked up sharply, hearing what sounded like a sneer in his brother's voice. "Well, yeah, I guess there have been some miracles. But I don't think our father was one of them. I don't think you should torture yourself wondering if Mom ended his life too soon, robbed him of some good years, if that's what's bothering you. I think she really did release him from his pain. At least, I have to think that's what he wanted. God, I'm going to miss him."

They both sipped their beers, not speaking, and then Greg broke the silence.

"Does Jill know about what Mom did?"

"No," Snapper said shortly. "I don't know why, but I couldn't bring myself to tell her. I don't quite know who I'm protecting—maybe both of them. Do you know that she asked to have Dad's eyes donated to this man she's been visiting in the hospital? I told her I'd have to talk to you. Mom isn't in a position to decide anything, but I suppose Dad would have liked it this way. He liked to give Jill anything she wanted."

Greg shrugged, puzzled by his own callous reaction. There was something so impulsively romantic about Jill that he couldn't help getting annoyed with her. Of course it was wonderful for this man, this stranger, to have their father's eyes. But she'd known the guy for a couple of weeks and already she was out to save his life. He was tired of seeing her get hurt. How well could she know this guy? Wasn't it dangerous for her to get so involved in his problems this way? Stifling his doubts, Greg said simply, "Sure, sounds good to me. But don't you think Jill has a right to know about Mom? She's going to find out sooner or later, and I don't know if it's the best thing for her if it's later. We all have a lot to deal with, but I think it's better if we stick together and face this as a family."

It was as though they had the same thought at the exact same moment. Snapper and Greg suddenly looked up and started speaking at once.

"What are we—"

"Do you think we should—"

They laughed, and the tension eased immediately.

"Were you going to say something about Mom?" Snapper asked.

"Yeah. I was going to ask you what you think we should do . . . can do, is more like it. What do you think, Snapper? Will she be all right?" Greg could hear the fear in his voice, and his stomach tightened. He wasn't ready to face any more bad news.

"I can't honestly say, Greg. Physically, she's in good shape and responding well to medication. But mentally she's suffered a severe shock. I think we might have to get her some treatment. I'm no psychiatrist, but I'd say she's very unwilling to let herself know what she's done. There's no telling how or what will get her to come back, to own up to what she did, then accept Daddy's death and get on with her life. That's a lot for her to deal with, and I think she's resisting it."

"Well, I vote we tell Jill and then take it from there. I'm in there with you on this." Greg raised his glass toward his brother in a mock salute, then tossed back the last of his beer.

* * *

Joanna pushed herself down into her bath until the fragrant bubbles tickled her nose. Lazily she gripped the elaborate hot-water faucet with the toes of her right foot and turned it on. The water grew even hotter, and her face began to tingle and steam in the heat. Sighing, she had to admit that she felt great.

When Jack had called her that afternoon asking if she would meet him for dinner, she was so surprised she'd been practically speechless. But she'd recovered quickly enough and made arrangements to meet him at a little out-of-the-way restaurant that they had discovered together on one of their drives. She was determined that Kay wasn't going to track her down this time, and Jack seemed just as interested in protecting their privacy. Which suited her just fine. She smiled to herself. She couldn't help her fantasies. Maybe it wasn't good for her, but she couldn't damn well help it.

But why in the world would a guy with a brand-new wife want to be meeting his ex-wife at a romantic restaurant? Jack had sounded strange on the phone, not at all his usual joking self. What she couldn't understand was why he'd seemed so amazed at having gotten hold of her. What had Kay been up to all this time? Joanna shook her head, frowning. That relationship had to end, and damn soon, too.

She glanced over at the small pink marble clock that sat on the dresser in the lavish bathroom, then sat up abruptly and began soaping herself. She wanted plenty of time to dress and get out of the house before Kay came back and started asking questions.

Forty-five minutes later, Joanna stepped back and twirled in front of the full-length mirror to get the effect of her outfit from every angle. She was wearing another new dress, a present from Kay. Crazy though the lady was, Joanna had to admit she had a great eye for clothes. This dress was a perfect shade of teal green that shimmered and changed to a blue gray in certain lights. The simple neckline, full sleeves and belted waist accented her curves and yet remained elegantly understated. She added a loop of glowing pearls and a pair of matching earrings. She was ready. For anything.

Soon she was sitting at a small table by the window, sipping on a dry vermouth and watching the moon gleam dully from behind the lacy network of wintry trees. The nervous fluttering in her stomach had begun as soon as she'd pulled into the parking lot and now had turned into an uncomfortable tightness in her chest. She took a sip of her drink and breathed deeply, trying to relax. It was only Jack. For Christ's sake, she had been married to the guy. And here she was acting like a teenager.

It was because she was hoping for so much. She had a feeling—she just had a feeling in her gut that Jack wasn't interested in getting together with her just to talk about how wonderful his new marriage was. Perhaps things weren't going so well, and she was suddenly beginning to look good to Jack again. If that was true, maybe it was going to be all right with her, and maybe not. But she sure as hell would like to have a choice in the matter.

All of a sudden she felt Jack's hand on her shoulder. She looked up and met his eyes for a long moment, and the tension inside her melted away. His eyes could always make her melt. Obviously that much hadn't changed.

"Hi, Jack," she said quietly.

"Hello, Joanna. God, you look beautiful." He

reached behind him to pull up his chair, unwilling to take his eyes off her for a moment. "Thank you for meeting me. I had to talk to you. I've been trying to reach you for days, but you were never there. At least that's what Kay said, but I could never figure out if she was lying or not. What's with her, anyway?"

"Oh, she thinks she's my mother or my keeper, or both." Joanna laughed, suddenly filled with a tingling feeling of lightness and freedom she hadn't felt in months. "You know, I think she's jealous. She doesn't like me to see any of my friends, but when it's a man—watch out. For all I know, she had a private detective follow me out here, and he's going to come bursting in here and embarrass us both. But you know, I don't really care."

"Yeah, you know, I don't think I care, either. Let's order. I'm starved."

How easily they slipped back into their old familiar patterns! It was comfortable being with someone who knew her so well, who remembered that she liked to order slowly, first course first and then the second course later, so they wouldn't be rushed. Jack ordered for both of them, a country pâté with warm crusty bread, followed by baked stuffed sole with a delicate lemon butter shallot sauce and crisp green string beans with almonds. He didn't even ask her about dessert, but ordered a split of champagne and a dense chocolate mousse that was so dark and fudgy it made them both gasp. Dessert had once been a sore point between them when she had been overweight. She had always ordered it defiantly, even when Jack had already called for the check. Now she waited to tense up and feel the same discomfort, but it wasn't there.

It wasn't just that she had lost weight and looked

different. Jack had changed, too. There was something more accepting about him, softer. He seemed more willing to listen. But right now it was Joanna's turn to listen.

As they sat over tiny cups of steaming espresso, Jack poured out the story of his marriage. He left out some of the details, but it was easy enough to understand the situation. It was strange, but Joanna felt no sense of jealousy or anger toward him or Peggy. He looked so sad and lost, like a little boy who had awakened to find that his favorite toy had been broken. But it wasn't only the child in him that touched her. In front of her sat a new, vulnerable man, someone who could admit that he was hurt—that he'd been wrong.

Joanna couldn't even count the times she had turned away from Jack, run to hide her own hurt and disillusionment when he had brushed her aside, impatient and unwilling to listen. Now he seemed unaware of how changed he was. He was talking about another woman, but it didn't matter. Peggy sounded like a wounded animal who had crawled so far back into her shell that no one would ever be able to reach her—not even her own husband.

Poor Peggy. Joanna had had no idea that her brutal rape had left her quite so scarred. She knew that Jack could sometimes be insensitive, but he certainly wasn't cruel. Impulsively, she reached out across the table and took his hand. "I'm sorry, Jack. It sounds terrible. For both of you." There was a silence as he returned the pressure of her hand, then gently turned it over so that it was cupped in his, her palm facing upward.

"It's been a nightmare, Joanna," he said softly, his fingertips tracing small circles on the sensitive skin of

77

her palm. "It's hard even to talk about it. And I don't know what to do. I really thought I loved her, but now I don't know. It's like trying to love a frightened child. She screams when I come near her, as though I'm her greatest nightmare come to life. It's a horrible feeling."

He gripped her hand tightly in his and averted his eyes. He opened his mouth as though about to speak, then stopped himself. Instead he looked up and smiled, gazing deeply into her eyes. "You're a beautiful woman, Joanna. You always were."

They had come in separate cars, but when Jack offered to drive her home and pick up her car the next day, she didn't protest. For two miles he drove without saying a word. Joanna glanced over at the familiar craggy profile, and her stomach tensed up again. She longed to snuggle over into Jack's shoulder and feel his arm tight around her; she remembered how they would sometimes drive for hours like that. She had to keep reminding herself that everything had changed. There was also nothing to be nervous about, she kept saying to herself, over and over.

When he pulled off to the side of the road, she wasn't surprised. The spot was familiar, a hidden driveway that led out by a field to a lake and an old deserted farmhouse. They had stopped here a million times before in their courting days. She had teased him, accusing him of being a bootlegger who kept his stash of moonshine at the old farmhouse. There had been a lot of jokes about the corruption of minors.

Now there was silence as Jack nosed the car so that it was facing the lake and cut the motor. He seemed reluctant to face her, suddenly shy after their intimacy in the restaurant.

She moved toward him first. "Jack, please look at me." Reaching out to him, she slid across the seat and suddenly found herself in his arms. It happened so quickly and felt so natural that she didn't have a moment to think. His lips covered hers, warm and sweet, his voice murmuring to her between kisses. She felt his strong hands on her back, and she didn't protest as he moved to unbutton her coat. For a brief moment she thought of Peggy, and then Kay. Wouldn't Kay throw a fit if she could see me now, she thought. And then she was lost again in a whirl of sensation.

Suddenly Jack pulled back. "You know that I'm still in love with you, don't you? I don't think I ever stopped. I don't know what happened with me. Peggy was something different. I don't quite understand it yet. But there was always a part of me that kept thinking of you, and wanting you. I'm sorry, Joanna, if I've hurt you."

Joanna couldn't speak as Jack took her face in his two hands and smothered her with kisses. This was so sudden—too sudden, protested a small inner voice. She knew she had never stopped loving Jack, but she had been forced to grow used to the idea that he belonged to another woman. And now suddenly he was saying it wasn't true. What was she supposed to believe?

Maybe the shock of being so rejected by a woman was enough to send him running back to what was familiar, comfortable. If that was the case, could she take him back? Oh, but she so wanted to believe him.

Jack's hand caressed her neck and moved slowly down her dress. His fingers were gentle, exploring, so exquisitely tender and wonderfully familiar—and yet something inside Joanna protested.

"No, Jack," she murmured. When her protests had no effect, she spoke more sharply. "Jack, stop. I think I'd better go home." Her hands felt shaky and she longed to be alone, to climb into her big bed in the Chancellor mansion—the closest thing to home these days—and just think. She needed to absorb all these new feelings about Jack. Somehow being this intimate with him after so long left her unable to feel, almost unable to breathe. She needed to think. Badly.

At her request, Jack stopped the car at the foot of the drive so that she could walk up to the house alone. As she moved to open the door, he put a hand out to stop her. "Joanna. I hope this wasn't too sudden. But you've been on my mind so much. Please think about what I said. I love you."

Unwilling to trust her voice, Joanna simply nodded and, gathering her bag and her coat, opened the car door and ran up the driveway toward the house.

Chapter Six

Conquest and Denial

Snapper walked next to his mother as a nurse wheeled her out to the waiting car. He and Greg and Jill had all planned to be there, to take their mother home. Now he was wondering if it was such a good idea. She looked great, almost like her normal self. But she still became so easily bewildered and unsure of where she was. Maybe having all of them there was just going to confuse her. Secretly, Snapper was hoping that having everyone around except Bill would somehow jog her memory, that she would suddenly remember her husband was gone and spare them the pain of having to tell her. When should he rip the veil from her eyes? He didn't know. None of them did.

Liz seemed thrilled to be home, to have all the old familiar things around her. It was almost as though suffering the stroke had wiped away all memory of the pain she had experienced in the past few months.

She went into the kitchen and opened the cupboard to get out her china teapot and teacups.

Snapper, Greg and Jill found themselves following her into the kitchen, looking at each other helplessly.

"Mom," said Snapper gently, "why don't you sit down and relax and let me do that. You really should get into bed and rest. You don't have your strength back yet, and you shouldn't overdo it. Here, let me take that." He took the tea things from her hand and led her to a chair. She sat down, suddenly bewildered.

"Where's Bill?" she asked anxiously. "He promised he'd come home in time for dinner tonight. Snapper," she said, taking his arm, "where is he? Do you know where Bill is?"

"Dad's not here, Mother," Jill said, stooping down in front of her chair and taking hold of her hands. Jill's brow was furrowed with worry, and she looked over at Greg and Snapper as though to see how she was doing. "The only thing you should worry about is getting better. You have to rest and let us take care of you. Daddy can't take care of you right now. You must just rest and try not to worry."

Liz stared at Jill like a trusting child. "He promised me he wouldn't be home late," she repeated, puzzled.

Snapper and Greg gently walked their mother into the living room while Jill brewed a pot of tea, automatically setting out a tray, cups, saucers and spoons and a pitcher of milk. How could this have happened? she wondered. It was as though the stroke, mild as it was, had allowed her to escape into a time warp . . . to return in her mind to the years when life had been easier for her to bear . . . to a time when her husband was still alive.

Jill poured hot water over the tea leaves and stirred the pot. It was uncomfortable seeing her mother like this. She was still so young and vibrant, a beautiful woman. And she'd looked so full of life on her wedding day such a short time ago. Now she seemed little more than a helpless child. The whole thing was a nightmare. What if their mother was lost forever in this never-never land, and they had to go on pretending that Dad was alive? Jill shuddered. Liz Foster was so much more than a mother to her; she was a close and dear friend, too. Losing her keen intelligence, her wit and warmth, would be too much to bear. She couldn't think about it. Hopefully, time would work its magic. Sometimes the body and the mind worked in mysterious ways to protect and nurture a person's physical and spiritual health. She would just have to trust that her mother was working things out in her own way.

Jill had to admit that part of her selfishly wanted her mother back so that she and David Mallory could meet. While her father was still alive, her mother could focus on nothing else. A couple of times Jill had broached the subject, mentioning that she had met someone new, but her mother had seemed not to hear her. She wanted her mother back, the warm, supportive, caring person she was—not this confused child.

In the living room, Snapper and Greg were sitting on the floor next to Liz's chair, almost like two small boys waiting to hear a bedtime story, Jill thought. Her heart went out to them—to all of them. Always Liz had been the strong one, pulling the family through the hard times when Bill had disappeared, sacrificing uncomplainingly, never letting anything get her down for too long. Now it was as though her reserves of strength and energy had abandoned her. How she wished they could rescue her somehow, reach her and make her realize that she still had so much to live for.

Jill remembered when her father first went away. The days and nights of puzzled waiting. Liz continuing to go through the daily routine as though nothing were wrong. Dinner on the table every night, her insistence that school work get done, classes attended and grades earned. It was only now, in retrospect, that Jill could really appreciate how strong she had been. Guiltily she remembered a conversation she'd had with her mother, accusing her of having driven their father away.

"Where's Daddy, then, if you didn't make him go away?" She remembered the venom in her voice, the uncontrollable fury she'd felt for her mother, who had calmly continued to stack dishes in the sink, never so much as flinching at the harsh words.

"I don't know where your father is, Jill. And I don't know what made him go away."

The tight, resigned note in her mother's voice had infuriated her still further. "Well, I know why he went away. He went away because of *you!* It's all your fault, and I wouldn't blame him if he never came back."

Her voice had risen to a shriek at the end, and she had raced upstairs to her bedroom and fallen on her bed, racked with sobs. Later she had wanted to apologize to her mother, to tell her that she hadn't really meant it. But it had scared her so much to see her mother coping, plodding ahead day after day. Somehow she knew that underneath the tough exterior her mother was scared, stretched tight as a wire, perhaps ready to break at any moment.

Maybe it wasn't fair that they had all forgiven Bill when he came back, Jill mused. But her mother loved him so much. He had always been her happiness, and their rejection of him wasn't going to change that.

As Jill poured out the tea she looked over to where Liz sat, her hands folded lightly in her lap. They had grown so much closer since that time. And now she so wanted, needed, to share with her mother how much she, Jill, had to live for. Because tomorrow David's bandages would be coming off.

The surgeons had performed the delicate cornea transplant immediately following her father's death, once permission had been given by the rest of her family. The doctors believed that the eight-hour operation had been a success, but the only way to really tell was when the bandages came off. The true test of the operation remained to be . . . seen.

Jill had mixed feelings about being with David tomorrow. Yesterday he had been so elated, so optimistic and happy, that it had scared her.

"Jill, in less than twenty-four hours I'm going to see your face. I can't believe it." David had reached out for her, finding her hands in that unerring way he had.

"Maybe you shouldn't get your hopes up too much," she'd said hesitantly, unwilling to squelch his excitement but worried about his brash optimism —afraid for both of them. "The doctors said the operation went well, but the outcome is still uncertain. Don't convince yourself that it was a one hundred percent success until you know for certain. I don't want you to be disappointed." Her voice had trailed away as she'd reached up to cup the side of his face with her hand. "But I'm praying, darling, I'm praying. It's just that I want it to work so badly I don't think I could stand it."

The next thing she knew, Jill had found herself in his arms. It was funny. She didn't think she'd ever had a relationship that had developed so quickly —and all at the side of a hospital bed. She wondered how she and David would get along in the real world. The hospital acted as a kind of cocoon, and David's illness as a kind of shared goal around which they had built a relationship. Jill had a hard time even imagining them out in the world together, going to dinner, movies . . . making love. Yet in some ways it seemed like the most natural thing in the world. She had never met a man quite like David. But there was still so much she didn't know about him.

The day before, she had questioned him about his family, feeling strangely uncomfortable.

"Why do you want to know?" he had asked playfully, refusing to respond to her serious tone.

"David, I've known you for weeks now, and I don't really know anything about you," she'd said, her voice rising slightly. "I know about the accident, but other than that I don't know a thing about you. Every time I get too close to something personal, you conveniently manage to switch the conversation back to me. You know everything about my past, starting from the moment I was born. I don't know the first thing about your life. Doesn't that seem strange?"

"Strange? No. There's really not that much to know, and I enjoy hearing you talk a lot more than I enjoy hearing me. Besides, isn't it more exciting to have a few secrets?" His voice was warm, teasing, and Jill had found it impossible not to respond.

"It's just that sometimes I feel that I've known you forever, and then suddenly I'll realize that I don't know about your family, or where you live, or whether . . ." She'd paused, embarrassed.

"Go on," he'd urged.

"Whether there are any other women in your life," she'd blurted out, feeling like a fool. But it wasn't all her imagination. Who was the stunning blond visitor that David had so conveniently avoided talking about when she'd asked? David Mallory might have a wife, a kid and three mistresses hidden away, for all she knew. Yet there was something so wonderfully honest and open about him—she believed in him intrinsically; somehow he inspired her trust. Or was it just that you tended to trust someone who was lying in a hospital bed with bandages over his eyes?

Nevertheless, she had to know for sure. It mattered very much whether there were any other women in David's life.

"You know, one of these days you're going to be walking out of this hospital and taking up your real life again. And I guess I'm just not sure what that life is all about." Jill knew she sounded defensive, but she couldn't help it. "I don't like surprises."

David laughed. "The only surprise you're going to have is getting used to a guy who can see again. When they take these bandages off, there's no telling what I might do." He grinned wolfishly and squeezed her hand.

"But where will you go? I don't even know where you live," Jill said plaintively.

"Don't worry so much. I'm a big boy now, you know. I'll be fine."

Jill felt the blood rush to her cheeks. She hadn't meant to pry where she didn't belong. It's just that it was so important to her to feel that she knew everything about this man. Maybe she was overreacting because of everything that had happened in the past. Her first marriage had been to a man in a hospital bed—a man who had never walked out of the hospital alive. Following the car accident, Phillip had lain in the hospital hovering between life and death. Yet during one lucid period he had insisted on marrying her in order to give the child she was carrying a name, a secure future. It had felt so strange to Jill, not quite right; but it had been Phillip Chancellor's wish, and she had agreed, realizing that it meant her baby would not be born into the world a penniless orphan.

Once this ordeal was over, she never wanted to stand next to a hospital bed again. She was ready for some joy in her life, some of the normal happiness that a woman should be able to expect when she was in love. Why was it that she seemed fatally drawn to situations that never quite gave her what she wanted?

This time would be different, she decided. But that's why it was so important to her to know everything about David. You're just jealous, Jill chided herself, hating to admit the truth. Face it, Jill Foster. You want this one all to yourself.

Joanna was walking on air. She woke up the morning following her dinner with Jack feeling as though the whole world had turned upside down overnight. Jack wanted her back. She knew it. Stretching luxuriously against the sleek satin sheets, she pulled her down quilt up around her chin. She was going to miss all this luxury, she admitted. As a college professor, Jack pulled in a decent living, but he was by no stretch of the imagination a rich man. She was going to have to get used to cutting corners again. It was surprising how easy it was to take luxury for granted, to accept all the little gifts—and all the not-so-little gifts. Kay was very generous that way . . . although Joanna sometimes wondered if she was being subtly bought. Usually she pushed those uncomfortable feelings to one side, unwilling to examine them too closely. To do otherwise would have meant forcing a confrontation, and with it the acknowledgment that it was time to leave. It was better to keep those disturbing thoughts somewhere in the background, particularly whenever Kay came home with a new box or bag.

But what the hell were clothes when she could be with the man she loved? Joanna stretched her arms back over her head, remembering their kiss last night. What had made her stop him, anyway? It had felt so wonderful, so incredibly right, to be in Jack's arms again. Yet something had stopped her from giving herself to him totally. Well, she had every right to be cautious, she told herself. In fact, she'd be a fool if she weren't.

Suddenly Kay burst into her bedroom, interrupting her reverie. She stormed over to the windows and jerked open the curtains, letting in a bright stream of early-morning sun.

"So tell me all about it," she said in a tight voice, angrily picking up the clothes that Joanna had strewn across the foot of her bed.

"Tell you all about what?" said Joanna, cautiously sitting up and reaching for her robe. This was going to be a bad one; she could feel it.

"You can start by telling me why the hell my car was delivered by a bartender from the Sleepy Bull this morning. Number one, why were you at the Sleepy Bull last night, presuming that you were. And number two, if you didn't need to drive the car home—then who, may I ask, *did* drive you home?"

God, the woman was incredible! Joanna had a

moment of sympathy for Kay's son, Brock. She must have been a terror to a kid growing up. No wonder Brock ran off to Europe and got into drugs. It was just amazing that he was such a sweet, generous guy, such a good friend. With a mother like Kay, he could have ended up a monster.

"I met a friend there for dinner," she said, hating the tight, apologetic note in her voice. "I had a couple of glasses of wine and didn't feel up to driving back. The roads are so dark out that way. My friend offered to drive me home and have the car delivered this morning. So I said yes."

Joanna noticed that she had carefully avoided referring to her friend as "he." And forget about telling Kay that she'd seen Jack. What was this thing Kay had about men? Was she so embittered by her own husband's infidelity that it had left her forever scarred when it came to the opposite sex? Was she always this jealous—or was it only with her?

"It was Jack, wasn't it," Kay said suddenly, turning from the closet where she was hanging up the crumpled teal dress. "You saw Jack last night." Her eyes narrowed as she walked toward Joanna and stopped at the side of the bed, looking down at her accusingly.

"As a matter of fact, yes, I did," said Joanna defiantly, unwilling to continue this charade for Kay's benefit. "He called and asked me if I'd meet him for dinner. He wanted to talk. He needed to talk to me." She found herself pleading with Kay.

"What kind of self-respect do you have, anyway, going off with a man who dropped you for another woman? Now he thinks he can come crawling back. And of course you're there waiting for him with open arms." Kay's voice was harsh, filled with bitterness.

"Men think they can do that. Tread all over you and then turn around and say they're sorry. You're a fool, Joanna."

"Kay, whatever your problem is, I'm not interested," Joanna said coldly. She climbed out of bed and walked over to the vanity and started brushing her hair. Behind her she saw Kay staring at her in the mirror, her eyes filled with a strange mixture of hate and love. "I've told you before. You don't own me. No one does. And the way I live my life and who I choose to see is my business. Do you understand that? I will do exactly as I please when it comes to Jack. You have no say in the matter. No say at all. Yes, I saw Jack last night." Her voice rose. "Yes, we had dinner. And I let him kiss me. He still wants me, Kay, and that's just fine with me."

She slammed the brush down on the vanity and, pushing past Kay, rushed into the bathroom and slammed the door. She leaned against it, her chest heaving. It was only then that she broke into racking sobs.

Chapter Seven

Pledge of the Heart

Liz was growing physically stronger every day, but when it came to facing up to the truth about her husband, she was still lost in her own private world of delusion. Somehow she had turned her focus, obsessively, toward her home, as though by repapering every room and hanging new curtains she could reverse the changes that had already shattered the fabric of her life. Despite her frenzy of activity, she still refused to set foot outside of the house, doing all her ordering and purchasing over the phone. Outside of her home lay danger, and illness, and loss. No wonder she wanted to stay indoors, thought Snapper sadly, where each object she looked at held at least one happy memory. No, as long as she was safe and sound in her own home, the truth wasn't going to find her.

Snapper, Jill and Greg took turns coming by to see her, once, twice, sometimes even three times a day. She would be sitting at the dining room table surrounded by books of wallpaper samples and swatches of material, jotting down measurements and lists on a yellow legal pad and jumping up every few minutes to run into another room with her tape measure. She seemed almost happy.

Was there any point in their breaking through this strange wall, Snapper wondered, only to have to cope with the pain and grief that lay on the other side?

Yet what kind of happiness did she really have? How many days, months, years could she hide behind wallpaper, fabrics and plans as though she were a young bride decorating her new home? They were running out of things to say to her and, more often than not, would sit opposite her at the dining room table, helplessly watching and listening as she chattered on.

"Snapper, I've decided to do your room in a pale ivory with very thin ice-green pinstripes. How does that sound?" She leafed busily through the book of wallpaper samples, pushing her glasses up on her nose. "I know you hate anything that's too busy. Remember when Daddy went out and bought that safari print wallpaper for your room? You loved animals so much, and he thought you'd be pleased to have your bedroom covered in lions and tigers and giraffes. But you hated it!" Her voice rose in a high, girlish giggle.

"You were so cute, Snap. Do you remember? You came downstairs and you were so solemn and you came over to me at the table—in fact, I think Stuart and Jennifer Brooks were over for dinner that night —and you pulled on my sleeve and you whispered in my ear, 'Mommy, I don't like the animals, they give me a headache!' So Greg ended up with the safari, and you got very tasteful off-white fabric wallpaper meant for the guest room. You had such sober, genteel tastes for such a little boy. Do you remember, Snap?" She looked up and stared at her son eagerly.

"Yes, Mom. I remember," Snapper said, grasping her hand and looking at her intently. "Mom. Listen to me. How *are* you? How are you feeling?" He lifted her hand to his lips and kissed it gently. "Can you talk to me a little bit?"

"Why, I feel fine, Snapper. Of course I'll talk to you." Liz pulled her hand away and rubbed it, puzzled, looking blankly down at the wallpaper samples strewn around her as though she suddenly couldn't understand what they were or why they were there. "What do you want to talk about?"

Snapper searched his mother's face and felt hot tears burn behind his eyelids. Where *was* she? She seemed fine, and yet she wasn't really there.

Yesterday, he, Greg and Jill had gone to see Dr. Vaughan, the same psychiatrist Jennifer Brooks had consulted when she'd first discovered she had cancer. If he treated a lot of cancer patients, they reasoned, perhaps he was experienced in dealing with the kind of extreme denial that their mother seemed to be suffering from, where reality was simply erased from the mind and replaced with a kind of blank cheeriness made up of fragments from the past.

Obviously, it would have been best if Liz had agreed to go and see him herself. But Snapper knew she would flatly refuse. She had always thought psychiatrists were a lot of bunk. If you had problems, you worked them out yourself, she'd always insisted. Now, stuck in a time warp that excluded even her own family, Snapper knew that trying to persuade her to see a doctor would be impossible—perhaps even destructive.

Dr. Vaughan had been patient and sympathetic but made no promises. What had they wanted to hear? That tomorrow morning she would wake up and be their mother again—strong, cheerful, confident, loving and totally there?

"She might 'come back,' so to speak, tomorrow, or next year, or maybe never," he'd said, leaning back in his chair and speaking slowly as he'd looked at each of them in turn. "In cases like this it's very difficult to predict.

"Your mother has lost what was most important in the world to her, her husband, and she lost him by her own hand. She has suffered a severe trauma that has left her no choice but to escape into a world where the implications of the choice she has made don't exist. She isn't catatonic; she can recognize and interact with her own children; she can probably be trusted not to harm herself and to function in a day-to-day fashion; but until she is ready to acknowledge the *fact* of Bill's death and her part in it, a portion of her memory has simply been erased in order to protect herself. That portion of her memory may return at any time—a memory, a phrase, would be enough to trigger it. Or it may never happen. I'm sorry that I can't be more definite. But your mother is a strong woman. I have every reason to believe that when she's ready to face life again, she will. She loves her children, and she seems to have had a good strong relationship with her husband. She probably isn't ready to escape from life forever. All I can tell you is to be patient, and give her time. Forcing the issue won't do any good—it will only drive her further into herself. The realization has to come from her."

It was hard to be patient, thought Snapper as he watched his mother busy herself again with her tape measure and calculations. He felt like grabbing her by the shoulders and shaking her. He wanted to see her cry, to scream, anything but this horrible, mindless chatter and blank-eyed cheerfulness. He wanted to scream at her, "He's dead! You killed him! Don't you remember!" and watch her face fall and crumple in acknowledgment.

It would be terrible, yes; frightening, yes. But at least it would be the truth.

Ever since their ugly confrontation following the night of Joanna's dinner with Jack, Kay had been acting like an angel. Sugar wouldn't melt in her mouth, Joanna thought suspiciously when she saw the rosebud in a silver vase on her breakfast tray or the latest gifts left for her in unexpected places—the beautiful new sweater sitting on the seat of the car and the amethyst pendant tucked inside the pages of the Sunday paper.

It was all too cute and coy for Joanna to be charmed at this late date. But it was also hard for her to turn down gifts—that was just a fact of life.

Joanna wasn't too hard on herself when it came to things like that. She wasn't about to lay judgments on herself when there was a whole world out there to do it for her. No, she'd had her share of hard knocks in life, and she should have some good things coming to her—she'd earned them. The fact was, she never felt guilty about taking things from people. Not that she felt like the world owed her or anything. She hated people who acted like that. But hey, if someone

Soaps & Serials™ Fans!

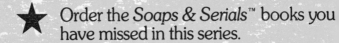 Order the *Soaps & Serials*™ books you have missed in this series.

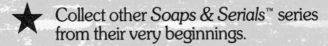 Collect other *Soaps & Serials*™ series from their very beginnings.

★ Give *Soaps & Serials*™ series as gifts to other fans.

...see other side for ordering information

You can now order previous titles of *Soaps & Serials*™ Books by mail!

Just complete the order form, detach, and send together with your check or money order payable to:

Soaps & Serials™
120 Brighton Road, Box 5201
Clifton, NJ 07015-5201

Please <u>circle</u> the book #'s you wish to order:

The Young and The Restless	1	2	3	4	5	6	7	8
Days of Our Lives......	1	2	3	4	5	6	7	8
Guiding Light	1	2	3	4	5	6	7	8
Another World.........	1	2	3	4	5	6	7	8
As The World Turns....	1	2	3	4	5	6	7	8
Dallas™................	1	2	3	4	5	6	7	8
Knots Landing™	1	2	3	4	5	6	7	8
Capitol™..............	1	2	3	4	NOT AVAILABLE			

Each book is $2.50 ($3.50 in Canada).

Total number of books
circled _____ × price above = $ _____

Sales tax (CT and NY residents only) $ _____

Shipping and Handling $ _____ .95

Total payment enclosed $ _____
(check or money orders only)

Name _____

Address _____ Apt# _____

City _____

State _____ Zip _____

Telephone (____) _____
Area code

YR 8

wanted to give her something, that was *their* problem, and it was just fine with her.

The trip to Hawaii was a different story. Her conversation with Kay had started a long time ago —in fact, Joanna was pretty sure that they had first discussed it at Bill and Liz's wedding, even before she'd come to live with Kay.

The Brookses had given Bill and Liz a honeymoon trip to Hawaii as a gift, and she and Kay had stood by the buffet talking about how much they'd like to go to Hawaii—in fact, maybe they'd even make the trip there together one day.

Ever since then, the Hawaii trip had become a kind of running joke. Whenever they were annoyed with each other, one of them would shrug and say, "Well, I guess Hawaii's off." Once, after a fight, Kay had even come home with a garish, oversize Hawaiian shirt and left it on Joanna's bed with a note pinned to it that said, "Forgive me. Just say the word, and we'll Aloha."

But two plane tickets and reservations at one of the swankiest hotels on Maui was taking the joke a little too far, Joanna thought. Sure, she'd give anything to lie around on the beach for a couple of weeks drinking rum and Cokes—well, maybe rum and Tab—and working on her tan. But with Kay? What kind of vacation would that be?

To be really honest with herself, the main reason she wasn't sure about the idea was the prospect of being alone with Kay in such romantic, intimate circumstances. Kay frightened her. So when Joanna walked downstairs that morning and found a pair of plane tickets, wrapped up in a hot-pink five-and-dime-store lei on the front hall table, she really didn't know how to feel.

But what was the worst that could possibly happen? Joanna didn't really think Kay would try anything . . . but she was so jealous and possessive. And after that last scene over her date with Jack, it seemed as if Kay had lost all sense of propriety about this. What did the woman want from her?

Joanna didn't know anything about those kinds of relationships between women, and she didn't want to. If she ever really thought Kay was like that, she'd leave in a second. No, Kay was just a lonely woman who happened to need a focus for all of her jealous attentions; that was all. And a vacation in Hawaii would be so nice. But now Kay's son, Brock, was making things even more confusing.

That afternoon, Joanna had been standing in the front hall twirling in front of the long mirror, admiring a negligee that Kay had bought for her. It was made of a shimmering silvery material that swirled beautifully when she moved, and it had a neckline that plunged almost to her waist. Joanna had lifted her hair off the nape of her neck to get the full effect when Brock had stuck his head inside the front door, making her jump. . . .

"Brock! I didn't hear the bell, you scared me!" Joanna twirled around, letting her hair fall down around her neck and the luxurious fabric of the nightgown wrap around her ankles.

Brock lowered his head in embarrassment and reached up to rub his short chestnut-brown hair with one large hand, taking a step as though to back out the door again. "I'm sorry," he mumbled, not looking at her, "I didn't mean to scare you. I came by to say hi to my mother, and I just didn't think. I'm sorry."

Recovering, Joanna reached out as though to draw

him back in, realizing with a desperate stab how starved she was for people, for company other than Kay, for the company of a man. "Wait, Brock, I'm sorry I screamed, but I'm always alone here, so I was surprised. Why don't you come in? Kay isn't here, but I could make us a cup of coffee and you could wait."

Brock moved tentatively into the hall. He had always been so gentle, thought Joanna, so unlike Kay that it was amazing to think they were mother and son. She remembered that horrible, unforgettable afternoon when she'd tried to take her own life after discovering that Jack wanted to—planned to—divorce her. If it hadn't been for Brock, she wouldn't be here now. He had found her, unconscious, on the bathroom floor, after she'd swallowed a bottle of sleeping pills, and he had rushed her to the hospital. He'd still been there when she'd awakened, feeling so bad that she thought she had died, and he'd stayed by her side to help talk her through the pain and humiliation.

He had persuaded her to try and hold on to her marriage, to give Jack another chance. It had also been his idea that she come and live with Kay.

It's funny, Joanna mused, looking at Brock now, how intimate you could be with someone, and how easily you could drift away again, to meet again almost as strangers. Maybe that's how you protected yourself from getting hurt too much—by taking yourself away from the people who reminded you of your greatest pain.

"So what do you think, Brock?" she asked flirtatiously, shaking off her own mood and twirling in front of him in the nightgown. "Doesn't your mother have good taste?"

Brock looked uncomfortable and started busily shuffling through the pile of letters on the gleaming oak table in the front entrance hall. "Yes, she does have good taste," he said, glancing up quickly and then down again. "But I think it's the wearer that does the gown justice, not the other way around."

"Why, that's very sweet of you," said Joanna, preening despite herself. Being slim was still too new a sensation for her to not soak up compliments like a thirsty sponge. "And flattery will get you everywhere." She laughed. "How about a cup of coffee?"

"No, I don't think so. I really should get going. Just tell Kay I dropped by, okay?" Brock turned and was out the door before Joanna could protest.

Why did he seem so uncomfortable? she wondered. Could he be *jealous?* No, Brock probably didn't have a jealous bone in his body . . . but you never could tell. Maybe all the attention and gifts Kay was lavishing on her wasn't quite what he had in mind when he'd dreamed up the idea of a live-in "companion" for his mother. Well, too bad, she thought almost angrily. She'd earned every last silk thread in this negligee with what she had to put up with from that crazy woman lately. No one, not even Kay's own son, was going to make her feel guilty.

Turning on her heel, Joanna stole one last backward glance at the lush folds of the nightgown in the mirror, then started up the stairs to change. Kay would be home for dinner soon. And God knows what little surprises she had dreamed up for tonight. . . .

Brock pulled out of the driveway, then almost immediately veered over to the side of the road and stopped the car. Resting both hands on the steering wheel, he stared out the window, frowning. He was worried, but he couldn't quite put his finger on why.

Kay was a hundred times happier now that Joanna was living with her—maybe that was just the problem. She was *too* happy, too preoccupied with Joanna, too wrapped up in her life. It wasn't quite natural. And what did all those gifts mean? Kay had never been loose with her money. In fact, quite the opposite. Brock remembered how hard it was to get her to buy anything—it was a little like pulling teeth.

He'd seen the two airline tickets lying on the front hall table. You didn't have to be deaf, dumb and blind to know who they were for. So why was his mother acting like a rich fairy godmother all of a sudden?

It wasn't that he didn't like Joanna. He cared a great deal about her. That was part of the problem, too. There was something about the whole setup that was a little suspicious. He had envisioned his mother living with someone who maybe cooked a meal for her once in a while, or took her for a walk, or went shopping with her on occasion. But this was ridiculous. Kay treated Joanna like she was her private property, almost like a *lover*.

Brock gripped the steering wheel tighter and shook his head. He couldn't believe what he was thinking. It was crazy, and it just wasn't possible. His own mother and *Joanna*? Maybe he was blowing this whole thing way out of proportion. Maybe Kay was so happy not to be alone that she was going a little overboard with the gift-giving bit. He would have a talk with her, try to make her see that she was making a fool of herself. He wouldn't use those words, of course. He'd do it gently, tactfully, try to persuade her to get out and meet some new people. Obviously, they just spent too much time alone together. That was the only problem. It could happen to any two people, that kind of dependency. He would talk to Joanna, too. She shouldn't be sitting around letting an older woman take care of her this way. It would be better for both of them if he stepped in and put a stop to this—and soon.

Satisfied, Brock started the car and pulled away from the curb. He had other things to worry about.

Peggy Brooks stared up at her bedroom ceiling, mentally tracing the whorls of textured cream paint with her fingertips. Her dark hair fanned out on the pillow, lank and unkempt. She wore a pair of sweat pants and an old shirt from high school days. The thought of changing clothes, brushing her hair or applying makeup seemed like too much effort to be worth it. The two beautiful dresses and the filmy nightgown she'd bought with such eager anticipation for her honeymoon were just a vague memory, the silly whim of some other woman. A stranger. A woman who had become a man's wife.

She didn't know how long she'd been lying there but felt no urge to rouse herself. Ever since she had left Jack and come back home, she'd hardly left her room. There didn't seem to be any reason to.

How comforting this room was, she thought, probably because it had hardly changed at all since she was a little girl. The wallpaper was the same, little blue forget-me-nots with a white background, and all her beloved books, the tattered bindings and pages coming loose, sat on the bookshelf undisturbed. She found herself picking up one book, then another, at different times during the day and slowly turning the pages, staring at the familiar pictures as though they might provide her with some answers. A row of stuffed animals sat on another shelf, staring blankly at her.

Peggy had wanted to take her favorite animal—a one-eyed bear with fur so worn that you could see the weave of the fabric underneath—along with her when she'd moved her belongings into Jack's house before their honeymoon.

She had battled long and hard with herself. *Don't be ridiculous,* said one voice. *Here you are going off to get married and you want to take along a stuffed animal you got when you were* four? *What kind of a baby are you, anyway?*

But what harm would it do? reasoned another voice. *You don't have to take him to bed with you or anything. He can sit in a closet and no one has to know, not even Jack.*

The battle had continued until she'd tucked the floppy, crooked little bear into her suitcase, then into one of her packing boxes, only to leave him at the last minute in his place on the shelf.

Maybe my marriage wouldn't have been such a disaster if I'd taken Teddy along, she thought, feeling hysterical laughter rise and bubble out of her. *Maybe he could have helped me through my wedding night—or better still, gone through it for me.*

Hugging the worn bear to her chest, she turned over on her side and buried her face into the old-fashioned tufted bedspread to stifle a harsh, wrenching sob. Her mother was lying in a hospital bed, dying, and here she was acting like a six-year-old, regretting that she hadn't taken a stuffed animal along on her honeymoon.

Peggy let her mind drift off again. It was the way she spent most of the day now—floating in a strange kind of mindless reverie. The sensation was oddly pleasant, almost narcotic, and she got annoyed when anyone interrupted her. Yesterday, her father had come upstairs and knocked on the door with her supper tray.

"Hi, Peggy, honey. How are you feeling? I didn't know if you felt like eating downstairs, so I had Sara fix you a tray. Do you mind if I stay and visit for a minute?"

Peggy saw the deep lines etched in his face, the dark, pained centers of his eyes, and her stomach knotted in response. *I'm letting him go through this alone*, she thought dully. *I'm not helping at all by being here with him. I'm only making it all worse.* For a moment she longed to fling herself into her father's arms, to bury her face into his shoulder the way she used to, to have him reassure her that everything was going to be all right.

But how could he? His wife, her mother, might have only a matter of days to live. How could he possibly tell her that everything was going to be fine? It wasn't going to be fine. Her mother was going to die.

"Thanks, Daddy," she mumbled, taking the tray and busying herself with folding and unfolding the napkin. She wasn't hungry; in fact, she could hardly remember the last time she'd eaten a proper meal. To please her father, she picked up the fork and poked at the food, rearranging it on the plate, wishing that he would leave.

"How are you feeling today, baby?" Stuart asked gently, easing down and sitting carefully at the end of her bed, as though he thought she might jump up and run away screaming if he got too close.

I must be acting crazy all right, Peggy told herself, then replied cheerfully, "I'm fine, Daddy. Just kind of tired, I guess. How are you?" She didn't want to ask the question that hovered in the air between them. *How's Mom?* They both knew the answer.

Peggy knew how much it would help her father to be able to talk to her right now. Of all his daughters, Peggy knew that he was especially close with her. They'd always talked about everything, and now, when he was going through the most difficult and painful ordeal of his life, she couldn't bring herself to reach out to him.

"Peggy, honey, I was wondering . . . that is, I thought maybe . . ." Stuart trailed off and looked pleadingly at Peggy, as though she might save him the pain and embarrassment of continuing. "I was wondering if you might like to, well, you know, see someone," he finished in a rush.

She knew what that awkward phrase "see someone" meant. When her mother wanted to see a psychiatrist, her father had balked at first. It had taken him a while to understand that Jennifer wanted to talk to someone outside the family just because she loved her family so much. "Stuart," she had said, "there are some problems that love alone can't solve. I have to talk this out. I have to."

Her father had finally come around and even gone along with Jennifer a few times to talk to Dr. Vaughan. Peggy knew that her father trusted him, had probably already gone to him to talk about her. Well, she didn't know if she wanted to. First of all, she couldn't imagine leaving her room, let alone talking to a total stranger. A man.

Even the thought of going downstairs seemed like too much.

Yesterday, she had ventured out as far as the third-floor landing just outside her bedroom, then had come scurrying back in and shut the door without even looking over the banister. It was almost as though she'd lost all sense of space and equilibrium. The world loomed large and dizzying out there; only in the four walls of her room, with her animals and her friendly old books, could she imagine living through the long days and even longer nights.

Last night she had torn herself awake again, screaming so loudly that her father had rushed down the hall to see if she was all right. The same nightmare had started to haunt her, recurring night after night until she was afraid to go to sleep.

The rape was happening, all over again, only this time in stark black and white and in agonizing slow motion. She opened her mouth to scream, but no sound came out. She strained and strained, calling Jack's name, begging him to help her. And just as she felt her scream welling up inside her, about to burst forth, she looked up and saw the faceless form above her take shape and turn into someone she knew. It was Jack who was raping her—her own husband.

She woke up screaming, drenched in sweat.

Stuart enjoyed his drives back and forth between the hospital and home. Maybe "enjoyed" was the wrong word, he thought sadly as he waited for the stream of traffic to break so he could pull out of Genoa General's parking lot. But it was the only time these days when he felt even slightly at peace.

He turned up the volume on the radio, and the sweet strains of a Beethoven violin concerto filled the car. One by one, as though they were strung as taught as wire and might snap, he felt the muscles in his neck and shoulders begin to relax.

Jennifer had been particularly bad today. Her eyes had barely responded when he'd walked in the room. They were dull, close to lifeless, and with a wrench he realized that the end was truly in sight. Intellectually, he knew what was happening, but emotionally he was far from accepting the truth.

The moments of anger were now mixed with a huge, bottomless despair. One minute he wanted to scream at her for daring to leave him; the next moment he wanted to pull her frail body to his own strong chest and try to breathe life and health back into her. But he did nothing—nothing but stand by the sterile white hospital bed each day and hold his wife's hand, trying to talk when she felt like it. Mostly, he just felt numb.

Automatically, Stuart began the drive home, letting the car carry him on the route that was by now nightmarishly familiar. The newspaper, once such an integral part of his life, had become a strange world to him these days. He stopped in at the office once in a while, just to make sure that things kept going, but his heart wasn't in it. The energy and excitement he usually got from putting out the paper had vanished. He wondered if he'd ever feel it again—ever feel anything again.

And now there was Peggy. Her lost, pinched face floated before him, and he pushed it away. It sounded callous, but he just couldn't give her his full attention right now. He'd tried to get through to her, but she just didn't respond. And it took every ounce of strength he possessed to be there for Jennifer.

Suddenly he thought of Liz Foster. He almost envied her, escaping into some strange, carefree world where reality didn't exist. But he missed her.

The bright, cheerful greetings she'd given him when he'd visited her the last few times had never quite reached her eyes.

He needed her friendship now, badly. She was one of the few people who could understand what he was going through, and she had deserted him, deserted the world.

It wasn't like Liz, he thought, feeling a stab of anger. Maybe everyone was just too accepting of her escape. Maybe all she needed was to be talked to, directly, like an adult. Her kids were treating her as if she were a helpless child or some fragile piece of crystal with a fatal crack.

Well, the Liz he knew was a different woman. She was gentle and tender, but she was strong. He thought back to the night when she'd asked him to come over and he'd listened to her sob, then held her in his arms. The Liz he'd held was vital and alive, a feeling human being, not this walking, talking puppet of herself.

Suddenly Stuart noticed that, without realizing it, he was heading toward the Foster home. Obviously, he had reached some kind of a decision. Maybe it was because his own daughter seemed so out of reach, beyond his help, right now.

But maybe, just maybe, if he reached out to Liz —she would reach back.

Chapter Eight

Desire's Awakening

Jill pushed open the door of David's room, her heart pounding. She'd been up since five that morning, unable to sleep, tossing and turning for an hour in bed, then finally giving up and pacing through the house, looking out at the garden from one window, then another, as a gentle dawn gave way to brilliant morning sunshine.

The hour she'd set aside for getting dressed had been ridiculously generous. She prepared carefully, buttoning the new dress of delicate peach linen and applying eye shadow, blush and lipstick with trembling fingers.

"He's going to be all right," she kept saying to herself, over and over again, in a half-whispered prayer. Even after brushing her hair, stroke after stroke, until it gleamed in soft waves about her shoulders, she still had an interminable half hour to wait before getting in the car for the ride to the hospital.

Now she walked over to his bedside, clutching her

purse until the knuckles showed white. David was sitting up in bed, looking no different from the way he did every other day. Maybe a little tense around the mouth, Jill thought, or maybe that was just her ridiculous imagination.

"Hello, darling. Good morning." Jill reached for David's hand and held it tightly in both of hers. "How are you feeling?"

Gently he brought her hands up to his lips. "I'm fine. I think how are *you* feeling is a better question. Did you sleep at all last night?"

"Well, maybe for a minute or two. How about you?" Jill laughed softly and pressed her fingers against his lips, feeling herself slowly relax as she always did around David. He was so strong, so sure. Even though their entire relationship had so far been conducted from his hospital bed, he still made her feel as though he were completely in control.

Not that he tried to control her. In fact, she sometimes wished during this difficult period of waiting that he were a little more demanding, a little less considerate and selfless. He was the one in the hospital; he was the one who had just undergone a terrible ordeal that could cost him his sight; yet more often than not he was the one who reassured her, gave her comfort.

"Well, let's see," David began in the slow, sexy drawl that always caught her right in the pit of her stomach. "I think, maybe somewhere in there between two and three in the morning, I might have caught a few short winks. Other than that, I've been counting a lot of sheep. Actually, honey, I slept surprisingly well. Dr. Savage came around early this morning to tell me that they're going to be taking the bandages off around noon today. And Snapper came by to wish me luck. You've got yourself a great brother there, kiddo."

David reached up and ran one large, strong hand down the side of her face, then back up again through her hair, lifting it and letting his fingers slide through the strands. Jill closed her eyes and leaned into his touch. She couldn't wait to see David outside the hospital, without a plastic hospital bracelet around his wrist, out of his hospital gown, dressed in a suit or in a pair of blue jeans—or with no clothes on at all, she thought, shivering suddenly in fear and excitement.

For weeks now she'd been dreaming of how it would be. David would arrive at her front door, and she would open it, wearing her long black silk kimono. Her hair would be flowing loose down her back, and her feet would be bare. She'd wear very little makeup. A bottle of Dom Pérignon would be chilled and waiting.

Slowly she would pull David into the living room and take off his jacket, her eyes never leaving his. Slowly, she'd loosen his tie and pull it out from under his collar. Very slowly, she would unbutton his shirt, first one button, then another. In her imagination, she could almost feel the dark hair curling soft and crisp on his chest, feel the powerful thud of his heartbeat as his mouth reached for hers . . .

Eleven-forty. In just twenty minutes the team of doctors would come through the door she'd just entered. They would stand around talking, discussing, consulting. She knew that David would sit there, calmly, his hands at his side, waiting. Already she could feel the frantic anticipation building inside her like a scream, threatening to spill over. Each minute now seemed like an eternity.

THE YOUNG AND THE RESTLESS

Jill stopped, suddenly realizing that she was pacing up and down next to David's bed. What help was she to him this way? She was acting as if it were her own fate that was about to be sealed in twenty minutes, not his. Well, in a way it was hers, too. She couldn't imagine life without David . . . but what if the operation was a failure? What then? Was she willing to tie herself to a man who would be dependent on her? Did she really care enough about David to be able to give her love, to give herself totally, to a blind man?

Right now, while the outcome of the operation was still uncertain, it was easy to say yes, to feel sure of her love. But what about in a month, or a year? Could she be so sure that she loved David that much? Yes, she thought fiercely, stopping at the foot of the bed and facing him. No matter what, she loved him. If David was blind, well, then she'd love him even more. She wasn't going to run out on this one. Her heart wouldn't let her.

Jack Curtis couldn't stop thinking about his ex-wife. In the middle of his Chaucer class, he found himself dreaming of how it had felt to look deeply into her eyes again, to kiss her full, soft mouth; he listened with only half an ear as one of his students happily brutalized the language of *The Canterbury Tales*.

Last night, he'd felt so restless and crazy, cooped up and pacing like some frustrated eighteen-year-old, that he'd gone out to a bar and proceeded to get roaring drunk. After the first couple of drinks he'd felt great, high and light and without a care in the world. But by the time he'd finished his fourth Scotch, the world was looking pretty bleak again. It always happened.

He had tried hard to put Peggy out of his mind, but suddenly images from his wedding night rushed in. Peggy's frightened, tear-streaked face, the ripped negligee, the boiling anger and disappointment in his gut that had made him see red. How much of what had happened was his fault? He knew she was afraid—had he not given her enough time or treated her as gently as he should have?

But he'd been treating her like some kind of vestal virgin for months, he thought defensively, giving her all the time in the world to work things through. He figured he'd been pretty understanding, listening when she wanted to talk about the rape, holding her when she just wanted to be held, even though he sometimes thought he would burst with the desire he'd been keeping in check for so many months.

He'd been a fool to think that marriage would change anything. How could a simple, silly ceremony heal wounds that went so deep? He'd been ridiculously naive to think that he, Jack Curtis, could just come along and erase that pain.

Was that what Peggy became to him somewhere along the way—a kind of crusade that provided him, noble gentleman that he was, with an opportunity to prove himself? Well, he had shown his true colors all right. The look of pure terror on Peggy's face when he'd left her in the hotel room that night was one he would never forget.

And now what? Suddenly Joanna had replaced all thoughts of his second wife, as though Peggy had never existed as a beautiful, desirable woman in his life. He'd thought he loved Peggy. He'd also loved Joanna once, too, and that feeling had drifted away as she'd changed, seeking solace in food, becoming unrecognizable as the beautiful young woman he'd fallen in love with. And now she was back, haunting his thoughts, in this enticing new incarnation.

The lovely, elegant woman who had been waiting for him at the Sleepy Bull the other night was almost a stranger—and yet still very much Joanna. She had the same quick humor, the same funny, warm smile that crinkled her nose, but she also possessed a new self-assurance, a kind of sexy independence that Jack had fallen head over heels in love with all over again.

But what did all this say about him? Was he incapable of loving just one woman? Was he going to spend the rest of his life falling in and out of love—failing at love?

The truth was, Jack couldn't stand the idea of being alone. Now that Peggy was gone, he found coming home to an empty house so lonely that more often than not he would go for a drive after finishing classes and usually end up at the local pub, where he stayed until closing.

What was happening to him? he'd ask himself more than once as he'd caught sight of his face in the mirror behind the bar. Who was this half-baked drunk who would stagger out at the end of an evening, practically knocking over stools and banging into doorways—who would arrive home and fall on his bed and into a deep sleep still dressed, only to wake in the middle of the night with a pounding head and a feeling of disaster in the pit of his stomach?

Out of guilt, Jack tried to visit Peggy once, wanting to reassure her that the marriage had been annulled. He figured that was the least he could do.

Stuart Brooks answered the door, and when he saw Jack his face disappeared behind a cold, angry mask.

"What do you want?" Stuart asked, his tone icy. "Peggy doesn't want to see you. You're not welcome here."

"I just came by to see how she's doing." Jack stumbled over his words, angry that he was allowing Stuart Brooks to intimidate him. "I just want to talk to her."

"No." The word was so hard and final that Jack felt as if the door had already been shut in his face.

Shrugging, he turned to leave. As he walked down the path, he turned back and glanced up at Peggy's bedroom window, wondering if she was looking down at him through the lacy curtains. Only five months ago he had driven back and forth in front of the Brooks home, trying to catch a glimpse of Peggy after she'd gone up to her bedroom, feeling more like an adolescent school boy than an English professor. That carefree, romantic gesture seemed like it belonged to another man, another lifetime, he thought, getting into his car and pulling away.

Much as he hated to admit it, he was relieved that Peggy's father had refused to let him see her. The simple truth was—he was afraid.

"All right, Mr. Mallory, I'd like you to keep very still. We're getting close now." Dr. Savage's voice was low and calm, contrasting sharply with Jill's state of nervous anticipation. Dr. Savage and his assistant had been unwinding the layers of gauze dressing from around David's head for what seemed like hours now. One of them slowly, gently lifted a layer of gauze, while the other folded each strip into loose folds and discarded it in a basin.

Jill marveled that David could remain so calm. Throughout the entire procedure, his hands had rested quietly at his sides, never clenching the blanket or in any other way indicating that he shared the mounting tension in the room. Jill, on the other hand, dug her nails into her palms until she felt a strange sticky dampness between her fingers and realized that she had drawn blood.

She tried not to hover too close behind the doctors, worried that she would be in the way. But more than anything in the world, she wanted to be the first thing David saw when his bandages were removed —that is, if the operation was a success.

It was so strange to think that David might now be able to see her, to actually look at her, and all because of her father's death. It wasn't as though David were going to be looking out of her father's actual eyes, but in a strange kind of way it was as if a part of him were living on in him.

Suddenly Jill was overwhelmed with tears. She gulped silently several times to try and calm herself. Daddy. In her anxiety about David, she'd had almost no time to dwell on her father's recent death. In fact, between helping with funeral arrangements, worrying about her mother and David's operation, she'd hardly had time to think about it. Maybe that was part of the reason she'd fallen so hard for David, she thought suddenly, and then pushed the thought away. No, fate didn't always choose its timing very carefully—or maybe meeting David right before her father's death *was* fate.

"All right, David, we're down to the final layer of bandages." The doctor's voice was calm and measured. "The light should be starting to filter through. Your sight will be very blurry at first, and the light will feel strange and painful. We've closed the shades and turned off the lights in the room, so it shouldn't be too bright. But don't worry if your vision is cloudy for a while. That's perfectly normal. It takes time for the eyes to readjust after being used to darkness for so long. Are you ready?"

"Jill?" For the first time since they'd started removing the bandages, David spoke. He reached out in her direction.

She moved over to the side of the bed and took his hand. "David?" she asked softly.

"Please stay here." His voice was controlled, but very low.

"Of course, David, I won't leave." She pressed his hand reassuringly. Her other hand, down at her side, was squeezed so tightly she thought her bones might break.

Stuart Brooks rang the bell of the Foster home and heard it echo inside. His heart jumped. He hadn't realized on the drive over quite how nervous he was. This is just Liz, he said to himself, trying to calm the feeling of nervous anticipation that bordered on fear. You've known Liz for more years than you can count. You've raised kids together. There's nothing to be afraid of.

Everything was finally getting to him.

Stuart had known for a while that Jennifer was going to die. But Peggy's marriage turning sour so suddenly and her mysterious return home had thrown him. He didn't know how to handle this one, and it made him feel Jennifer's absence more profoundly than ever.

On his last visit to the hospital, he'd tried to bring up the subject subtly, in a way that wouldn't get her overly concerned.

"Jen, hon," he'd said softly, standing by her bedside and hunching over so that he could hear her whispered replies, "Peggy's back home. I thought you'd want to know."

"Peggy?" Her look had been vague, almost blank, and his heart had sunk.

"Yes, dear. You remember that Peggy left to get married, but she's come home to stay for a while." He'd seen her struggling through the drugged mists to figure out the meaning of his words. She'd resisted taking medication for so long, but eventually the pain had grown so intense that it had burned out of her eyes . . . and she'd succumbed.

Now that she'd finally started taking the pills, the feverish brightness was gone, replaced by a dull shadow, as though a filmy curtain had been pulled down over the brilliant, laughing blue eyes he so loved.

It wasn't that Jennifer didn't know who he or her daughters were, exactly. But sometimes the medication seemed to erase her memory of the present and send her back in time. Other times he arrived to find her as intensely awake and lucid as she'd always been. It was disarming not to know ahead of time which state she'd be in, and now he had the same feeling about Liz. Not that she was bedridden and in pain, like Jennifer, but he knew that she'd been refusing to face reality for a while.

Stuart heard quick, light footsteps in the hall and stepped back as the door burst open.

"Stu!" Liz smiled widely and threw her arms around him in a big hug. "What a wonderful surprise. Come in! Come in! I was just making a cup of coffee. You must come and see what I've been doing. I've been so naughty! You know Bill and I never can agree on how to do the house, but this time I've just put my foot down. I've been wildly extravagant! Paterson's delivered all the wallpaper and paint this morning, and the workmen are going to be starting on the upstairs in the morning. Isn't it exciting? You and Jennifer and the girls will have to come over when it's all done and we'll have an open house."

Stuart followed Liz on her path to the kitchen as she chattered on, pointing out rolls of wallpaper and buckets of semigloss. The house was in a state of chaos. There were half-full lunch dishes on the dining room table, as though she'd been in the middle of a meal and suddenly forgotten that she was eating. The kitchen was covered in buckets and mops and bottles of ammonia and cleansers, as though she'd suddenly decided to add spring cleaning to her list of projects. It wasn't a chaos of neglect, thought Stuart. It was the chaos of a woman who was running from something so hard that she'd just about run herself out.

"Liz," he said gently, taking her arm. "Forget the coffee. Let's go sit down."

With the same manic force that had been driving her, Liz's mood of cheery exuberance suddenly vanished. Stuart felt her whole body droop, as if she'd been holding tight to a rope and suddenly let go. For some reason, it made him feel strong again.

He led her into the living room, where gentle afternoon sunlight filtered in and turned a burnt-orange corner love seat into warm gold. He led her to it, supporting her arm until she was seated. Then he sat down next to her and took both her hands in his. They were slightly rough, still warm and damp from being submerged in water. It made his heart wrench.

This was where Liz was finding her comfort—in a bucket of soapy water and a scrub brush. Well, there were worse ways to fight off demons.

"Liz, I've just come from seeing Jennifer at the hospital." He looked directly into her eyes and held them with his, hardly daring to breathe. He didn't really know what he was doing, but he was following a hunch. He knew this lady, and he just hoped he wasn't wrong.

"What's happened? Why is Jennifer in the hospital?" Liz's voice rose in panic. She began to pluck at the fabric of the love seat with her fingers.

"Jennifer's sick, Liz. You know that. She's been in the hospital for a while now. Remember, she went in right after Bill did." Stuart took both of her hands in his and squeezed them hard.

"Bill . . . Jennifer . . . in the hospital. . . . What do . . . I don't . . . understand. . . . What are you talking about?"

Her mouth began to work, struggling for words. She pulled her hands from his and started rhythmically smoothing the hair back from her forehead. "You're wrong. Bill's here . . . he's home. We're . . . redecorating. I'm picking out wallpaper . . . and . . . and Bill is helping me. He's just not here now. I don't know where he is. . . . Maybe Snapper . . . Greg. I don't know where he is now. . . ." She trailed off and started looking around frantically, as though her husband might walk in any minute.

Stuart felt a lump rise in his throat and he longed to take her in his arms and soothe her, tell her to forget what he'd just said. But he didn't speak. Instead, he sat and watched her intently, praying that he was doing the right thing.

It would kill him to think that Liz might be in too

fragile a mental state to endure his telling the truth —that he was helping to push her over the edge. But he'd built the best newspaper for five counties around by going with his hunches, and he wasn't about to abandon his intuition now.

"Liz," he began again, gently, trying to catch and hold her eyes with his. "Liz, do you remember when Bill went into the hospital? Do you remember that Bill was very, very sick?"

She lowered her hand from her hair and slowly looked up at him, searching his face.

"Bill . . . sick? Bill . . . sick . . . Bill . . ." Suddenly her face crumpled, and a low moan came from deep inside her chest. She began to sob, pounding Stuart's chest with both fists, her face twisted with shock and grief.

"No! No! No! No!" Her words were a harsh chant that kept time with her fists. Stuart didn't stop her, letting the strength of her balled hands reverberate through his body. Then, with a long, loud wail and one last blow to his chest that seemed to use up the last of her strength, Liz collapsed onto the sofa, burying her head in her hands. Stuart let her cry, remembering the night she had cried out her rage and her fear—and then quieted. He hoped that the same release would follow now.

Stuart didn't know how much time passed. Long shadows filled the living room and there was a chill in the air. His body felt stiff with tension, from sitting in one position for so long, but he was reluctant to move.

Liz's sobs had quieted to an occasional gentle moan interspersed with a soft hiccuping sound. Her gold hair, lightly peppered with gray, was fanned out across the sofa. Stuart waited.

Suddenly she sat up, her face streaked with tears and smudges of dirt. She spoke in a calm, almost cold voice. "I know Bill's dead, Stuart. I know. I killed him."

The tension escaped his body as though a balloon had burst. With a sob that caught painfully in his throat, he held out his arms. "Oh, Liz, I'm sorry. I'm so sorry."

Gently, as though to make up for the blows she'd rained on his chest, Liz lowered her head to his chest and closed her eyes. They sat together in the living room, not moving, holding each other until darkness closed in.

Jill felt David's hand tighten on hers. She looked down and traced the strong fingers where the knuckles were white with tension. The dark hair on his tanned forearm contrasted sharply with the white hospital sheets. Jill traced a blue vein that pulsed imperceptibly in his wrist. It filled her with a helpless tenderness, and again she had to blink back the tears. He was so strong, she thought, but he had to be feeling like a frightened kid inside.

Slowly, Dr. Savage and his assistant began to remove the final layer of gauze. Jill covered her mouth with her hands to stifle any sound. The skin around David's eyes was puffy and bruised a light purple, as though he had two black eyes. With a start, she noticed the dark curve of his lashes against the tender, mottled skin. They trembled, and his eyes oozed tears in a reaction to the dim daylight that filtered into the room. Slowly, his eyes flickered open. They were so bloodshot that she could hardly tell their color. He looked as though he'd been the sole survivor of a terrible barroom brawl, she thought tremulously. For a second his eyes remained open, then they dropped shut again.

"David . . ." Jill moved in front of him and reached out to touch his face. "Darling . . ."

Suddenly David pulled his hand from hers and sat up straight in bed. "I see something," he said in a tense voice. "I think I see light and flickering —something." The muscle in his jaw twitched beneath the shadow of his beard. "Doctor, I think I see something."

This time, getting used to the light, David kept his eyes open. He blinked once, twice, and then managed to focus. For the very first time, Jill was looking into his eyes.

Suddenly David bowed his head, tucking his chin into his chest. Jill felt her heart flip-flop in fear. What was wrong? Had the operation failed? She held her breath.

Then David looked up again. Through the blood-red whites of his eyes, Jill could see at the very center two pinpoints of light. Slowly he opened his mouth to speak.

"I can see you, Jill," he said in a low, husky voice. "I can see you, and damn it, you're beautiful."

Chapter Nine

Sweet Betrayal

Joanna pushed herself deeper into her lounge chair and sighed impatiently, continuing to flake the polish from the nails of her right hand. She was scheduled to have a manicure that afternoon, so she really didn't care what state her nails were in. Maybe she'd get some kind of outrageous color today—vampire red or fuchsia orchid. Kay hated anything but very pale pink or clear polish, but Jill was in a mood to go out of her way *not* to cater to Miss High and Mighty's good taste. Besides, Jack thought red nails looked sexy. "Nothing like getting a pair of long red nails raked down your back," he used to say, teasing her about her unmanicured hands.

Well, times had changed since then. *That* was the understatement of the year, she thought sadly as she watched a tall, lean young man execute a neat jack-knife off the diving board. Here she was, sitting at the old lady's club, watching all these nice specimens of manhood prancing in front of her, and she couldn't do a thing about it. Because Kay was her meal ticket right now—and it wasn't smart to cheat on your free ride.

For a moment she felt a pang of remorse. She didn't really like feeling this way about Kay. But lately things seemed so out of control, so out of her reach.

Jack filled her waking thoughts and her dreams. Last night she'd dreamed that they were walking together on a beach, hand in hand, into a huge sun that got bigger and hotter and more golden the farther they walked, until it was so huge that it filled the sky, burning the sand under their bare feet. She'd awakened tangled up in her sheets, gasping for air as though she were drowning.

Joanna knew she couldn't go on like this much longer. She felt as if she were in some kind of limbo state, suspended between Kay and Jack, with Brock looking on like some disapproving older brother.

Maybe she should just ditch everyone and get a place of her own, get a job and enjoy a little independence. She could cut back if she had to. She had enough new clothes to last the next five years—that is, unless Kay decided to reclaim the merchandise in the divorce, she thought bitterly.

The little scene they'd had that morning was just about the last straw, Joanna thought, reaching down into her canvas tote bag for a cigarette. Recently she'd started smoking again—a bad sign—although not when Kay was around, of course. It gave little ol' Kay a sinus headache. Well, at least she wasn't stuffing her face. Contentedly she blew a plume of smoke toward the vaulted ceiling of the pool and looked down at her flat stomach, which hardly strained the thin material of her swimsuit.

She and Kay had been sitting at the dining room table with travel books and maps spread around them, making plans for their trip to Hawaii, when Brock came bursting in. He hadn't even looked at Joanna but stood over his mother's chair, glaring down at her, his hands on his hips. . . .

"I want to talk to you." His voice was flat but held a dangerous edge. "Alone."

Joanna had never seen him look so angry. He really is a handsome guy, she thought, cocking her head and eyeing him with detached amusement. "Well, I guess I'll just go into the other room and make myself some iced tea," she cooed, knowing that the voice would infuriate both of them.

Given how dull things were getting around the place, she was almost enjoying this confrontation, she realized, amused. She put on the kettle and opened and closed cupboard doors in her search for tea bags, making just enough noise to be convincing, but not enough to drown out the voices in the other room. She didn't have to try too hard: the voices were rising.

"Mom, I can't understand you. You're making a complete fool of yourself."

"What on earth do you mean, Brock?" Kay's voice was flat, not the trace of a question in her reply.

Joanna gave in to impulse, tiptoed over to the doors that separated the dining room from the kitchen and peered into the other room through the diamond pane in the upper part of the swinging door. Kay was looking up at her son with a small, self-satisfied smile on her face.

"You're spending all your money on clothes for her, and now you're going to Hawaii. What kind of fool do you think she takes you for, anyway? Obviously she doesn't care about you. All she cares about is your money."

Brock's face was twisted in anger and frustration, and for a moment Joanna felt a pang of regret. She cared for Brock and had thought he cared for her, too, but her relationship with Kay seemed to be getting to him. In a big way.

"Besides," he blurted out, "it's not natural the way you spend so much time with her, buying things for her."

So that was it. Brock was jealous. But inside Joanna's head, his words echoed eerily. Hadn't she felt the exact same way about things? Wasn't Brock giving voice to her own fears? Hadn't she felt plenty of times that Kay's interest in her was not quite . . . normal? And wasn't she left feeling, when all was said and done, after all the attention Kay paid her, the shower of gifts, that she was smothering . . . drowning . . .

Kay was standing now, her hands placed on the back of one of the elegant Chippendale dining room chairs, her head lifted haughtily.

"I don't know what's gotten into you, Brock, but if I didn't know you better, I'd say you were jealous! My, my, my, isn't *this* a surprise." Kay's smile was tight and triumphant. Joanna shuddered. It was disquieting to be standing in the kitchen, peering out through the door like some kind of scullery maid or something, hearing herself being discussed as if she were a piece of merchandise.

"Brock, my dear, the way I choose to spend my money is entirely up to me. Besides, it gives me something to do with my time." She began gathering the gaily colored maps and brochures into a neat pile, ignoring her son.

With a chill, Joanna looked around the kitchen, suddenly feeling trapped. Something about Brock's visit disturbed her. Maybe it was hearing her own thoughts come out of his mouth, as if she'd spoken them. Maybe it was seeing the cold, proprietary way that Kay discussed her—*her*—with someone else.

"Yeah," she suddenly heard Brock snarl bitterly, "that's all you've ever had to give, is time. Funny I never saw any of it."

Joanna's heart wrenched at the anguish and fury she heard in his voice. He sounded more like a wounded little boy than a grown man. On impulse, she pushed open the swinging doors and entered the dining room.

"Kay . . . Brock . . ." She trailed off, not quite sure what to say. "Hey, you two, what's all this bickering about?" She tried to make her tone light, hoping to break the tension that vibrated between mother and son like a wire stretched to the breaking point.

"Stay out of this, Joanna. This is none of your business." Kay's voice came like a slap in the face. Joanna gasped. She'd never heard Kay quite like this, her voice dripping with icy venom. This cold, angry woman was formidable.

Something in Joanna protested.

. "What do you mean, stay out of this? I'm not your child, Kay. You were talking about me, and I have every right to hear what you're saying." The blood pounded behind Joanna's temples.

Brock stood staring first at his mother, then at Kay, the muscle in his jaw working furiously. Then he turned and stormed out the front door.

Kay, continuing to organize the brochures, said in a voice that now seemed to drip honey, "Joanna, precious, where shall we go for dinner tonight? I'm in the mood for some really good seafood. How about you? You know, we should try that new little place they opened up downtown, I think it's called the

Boatslip. They're supposed to have wonderful stuffed sole. . . ."

Stubbing out her cigarette in one of the molded plastic ashtrays provided by the club, Joanna sighed and closed her eyes. After the scene with Brock, she'd turned and walked out on Kay, unable to speak she was so angry, and driven blindly to the pool to give herself time to think—alone. But even though she'd cooled down by now, her thoughts were still pretty disturbing.

Hawaii or no Hawaii, dresses or no dresses—she'd had enough. She wanted out. The way Kay had talked to her own son made Joanna's blood run cold. She'd always assumed that beneath that selfish, difficult exterior, Kay had a good heart. Sure, Joanna knew that Kay had been a heavy drinker once, and that she'd turned a lot of people against her, but treating her own son as if he were a stranger was unforgivable. How could she have lived with a woman like that for so long?

As soon as the thought of leaving—really leaving —entered her mind, Joanna felt a terrible sense of urgency. She knew she didn't have enough money to make it on her own right now, and getting a job at the drop of a hat wasn't always so easy. But that didn't matter. What was important was getting out of Kay's house . . . out of Kay's clutches. . . . Jack. Joanna sat up so abruptly that the young man poised to dive by the side of the pool turned to stare. She would go and see Jack. That's what she'd do. She'd go this afternoon, straight from the club. If he really felt about her the way he said he did, he would help her. She knew he would. They could go together back to Kay's house to pick up her things.

He'd told her that his marriage to Peggy had been

annulled, so he was free again. Her ex-husband was free.

Joanna bit her lip nervously. Maybe he was free to be hers once more.

Jack Curtis was furious. He'd called the Chancellor home five times already that morning trying to reach Joanna, and each time the maid had answered in the now familiar monotone, "I'm sorry, she's not able to come to the phone right now." Jack wanted to throttle her but instead let loose with a stream of expletives. The next time he called and said hello, the person on the other end hung up before he could say a word.

Kay Chancellor was off her rocker. Did she actually think she could get away with keeping someone a virtual prisoner? Jack was about to lift the receiver again, when he thought better of it. Slamming the phone back in its cradle, he grabbed his jacket and left the house, banging the door behind him.

If Kay thought she was going to stop him from seeing Joanna, she had another thing coming. Jack hadn't been able to see or talk to Joanna since the day of their dinner, and it was driving him crazy. He couldn't think of anything else, and if he didn't get to see her *today*, someone was going to pay for it. And it looked like that someone was going to be Kay Chancellor.

He stood in front of the imposing front door and pushed hard on the bell, keeping his finger there. He heard the bell ring long and shrill inside. Kay had been driving him crazy, so he figured it was about time he returned the favor. He kept pressing.

Suddenly the door was flung open and Jack found himself face to face with Kay. She was dressed in a well-tailored black suit and was carrying a black leather clutch bag in her hand, as though she'd been about to go out.

"Yes, Mr. Curtis, what may I do for you?" Her voice was cool and detached, completely devoid of feeling.

"Yes, you meddling old witch, you can do something for me." Jack felt the blood boil behind his eyes. All the anger of the past week seemed suddenly to spill out of him, and it took every bit of restraint he possessed not to take the collar of her expensive tailored suit in both his fists and bring her face up close to his.

"You can start by telling me why you haven't let Joanna take any of my calls, and why you never even told her that I had called. Next, you can tell me what gives you the right to keep her here practically under armed guard. And last but not least, you can let me in so that I can see for myself where you're hiding her."

Jack started to move past Kay through the front door, but she stepped in his path, putting one linen-clad arm out to bar his path.

"I wouldn't do that if I were you, Mr. Curtis. There's this little law we have in Genoa City. I think what you're doing is called trespassing."

Unable to hold himself back, Jack grabbed her arm and then just as suddenly released it. What on earth was he doing? The last thing in the world he—or Joanna, for that matter—needed was to get Kay really angry. She was a cool cookie and wielded a lot of power in this town. Given the nature of small-town politics, he wouldn't be surprised if Kay Chancellor had something to do with every important business in Genoa City—she was probably even a force behind the board of directors of the university. He was up for tenure in just two months. Did he really want to risk it by letting this crazy woman make him do something foolish?

No. He and Joanna would figure something out. Joanna was a grown woman, able to come and go as she pleased. It was crazy to even think that Kay was keeping her a prisoner here. What did he think this was, some kind of gothic horror novel or something? Kay Chancellor was just a jealous, embittered woman who took what she wanted and didn't ask questions. But she didn't own Joanna.

He turned on his heel, leaving Kay standing at her front door. Joanna would come to him when she was ready, Jack reassured himself. Of that much he was sure.

Jill stood staring out the window of David's hospital room to the parking lot below. In just a few minutes she and David would be walking out together—a moment she'd dreamed of practically since she'd met him. So why wasn't she feeling happier?

She turned her head and looked over to where David was packing his things into the small overnight case that lay open on the bed. He was wearing a pair of slacks, an open-necked shirt and a sports jacket, the clothes he'd had on when he came to the hospital close to six weeks ago. Even with his bruised eyes, David looked very handsome—and very sure of himself.

She'd known him all these weeks—six, to be exact. Why was she all of a sudden feeling so shy and tongue-tied? She'd hardly been able to put two sentences together since she'd arrived that morning to pick him up.

Jill knew exactly what her fears were based on.

While David had been lying in a hospital bed, his world was defined by the four walls of his room; he was a known quantity. But now that he had his sight back and was well on the road to a full recovery, he was heading out into the world again, to pick up the threads of his life—a life that Jill knew almost nothing about. What she also didn't know was where she was going to fit into that life—or whether David even wanted her there.

She had awakened that morning in a panic, her mind churning. What if David, underneath his warm, charming exterior, had really been using her all this time? What if she'd only been an interlude to him, a companion to make his time at the hospital more pleasant—or worse, simply a way to get hold of the cornea he so desperately needed?

Angrily, she'd pushed all the nagging suspicions aside, punching her pillow into a more comfortable shape and turning over on her other side.

Of course David was sincere; he just wasn't the kind of person to talk about himself nonstop. That's why she didn't know much about him. Besides, why would he bother carrying out the charade of falling in love with her all these weeks if he didn't really mean it? Either he really was sincere, or he should be up for the Academy Award as best actor in a real-life drama.

It was Snapper and Greg who had raised a lot of the doubts that were now nagging at her. She'd tried not to listen to them, but it was difficult after so many years of looking up to her brothers. They'd all gotten together to have dinner the night before, and the conversation had drifted to David Mallory. . . .

"I'm glad he got Dad's eyes, Jill, but how much do you really know about this guy?" Greg asked, looking at her intently. "He's good-looking, and he seems like a nice guy, but that's not reason enough to give yourself to him blindly. Sorry, no pun intended, but you know what I mean." Greg took a long sip from his beer and looked to Snapper for agreement.

"I have to say I'm with him, Jill. I like the guy, you know that. And letting him have Dad's eyes was fine—I think Dad would have liked that. But we're just concerned that you're rushing into something again before you know what you're doing. We don't want you to get hurt, and you don't really know anything about Mallory, do you?"

Jill shook her head and continued to make overlapping circles on the paper place mat with the base of her wineglass. She knew she didn't have an answer that would satisfy them. And in a way, they were right. She didn't know very much about David. He *was* almost a total stranger. But that didn't seem to matter. She knew what she felt about him in her gut, in her heart. And that feeling inside told her everything she needed to know about him. The facts could come later, once she knew him better.

Of course, she didn't expect that he'd had no other life, no other women before he'd entered the hospital. That would be ridiculous. But weren't her brothers getting a little carried away? She was a grown woman and could take care of herself now.

Or did they know something about David Mallory that she didn't?

"I appreciate your concern, both of you. Believe me, I really do. I know you mean well. But what I feel about David Mallory is my business. I admit I don't know a lot about his life yet, but I plan to," she rushed on. "That will take a little time, and I don't want to push him. He's been through a terrible ordeal, and the last thing in the world I want to do is start bugging him about commitment and stuff like that. He needs time. I need time. All I know is that I love him."

Snapper and Greg were silent.

"Look," she continued, "I know you probably feel responsible for me because Daddy died so recently and everything. But it's really not just about his death—a reaction to it or something. Truly, I've thought about that a lot, wondering if that's partly why I fell for him, now, right around the time Daddy went into the hospital. All I know is that I've never felt like this before—about anyone. And I'm going to keep seeing David no matter what you or . . . or Mom, or anyone else thinks."

Snapper cleared his throat and signaled to the waitress for the check. "Jill, it's not that we don't trust you. You know that. I guess maybe we're feeling a little overprotective, since Mom and everything. Maybe we're getting things confused. Just promise me one thing—that you'll go slow, not rush into things. Give David some time to readjust to life outside the hospital. Okay?" He reached out and took her hand across the table.

Tears pricked her eyes. She loved her brothers, and they'd been through so much lately. "Of course I promise. I love you, both of you," she said. "Let's just keep sticking together, okay?" She reached out with her free hand to Greg, and for a moment the three of them just sat there, holding tightly, reassuringly, to one another. . . .

Now, waiting for David to finish packing, she tried to recapture the confidence she had felt talking to her brothers. She was about to walk out of the hospital with David Mallory, out into the world—hopefully into their future.

And she was scared.

* * *

Joanna climbed out of the cab in front of what used to be her home and turned to watch as the driver pulled away. She felt naked, exposed, standing out here with just her little canvas tote bag, wearing nothing but a pair of blue jeans, a sweat shirt and running shoes, her hair still clinging in damp tendrils to the back of her neck from the humidity at the pool.

Here she was, she thought ironically, a damsel in distress coming to throw herself on the mercy of her ex-husband. Well, it really wasn't anything quite that dramatic. More like trying to look up an old friend in time of trouble.

No. She had to admit it: it was a lot more than that.

Mrs. Harper, Jack's nosy neighbor, was probably getting an eyeful right now, she thought, amused. Enough to keep the neighborhood hotlines burning for hours. Well, hopefully she'd give them something to *really* talk about soon.

She remembered the early days right after their honeymoon, when the struggling English professor and his eager young bride had cavorted around like a couple of puppies. She could hardly remember ever getting dressed during that time, she thought with a smile, and when she did it was usually in some filmy, lacy concoction that didn't deserve to be called a piece of clothing.

They'd made love more times than Joanna had thought was humanly possible. Jack was a considerate, wonderful teacher, and she'd been a pretty willing pupil. After a long afternoon of making love, Joanna would give up her lacy nightie in exchange for one of Jack's old shirts, and rolling up the sleeves, she'd go into the kitchen to throw herself into cooking. They were always ravenous back then, she remembered. She would cook up a huge pot of pasta with a rich sauce made of butter and cream and cheese, and they'd wolf it down with hunks of bread and a bottle of red wine—and still have room for ice cream.

Those happy, carefree days seemed like a million years ago.

How strange it felt to be ringing the doorbell of this house, as though she'd never lived here. But then, she'd thought once that she might never set eyes on the place again—so what was really so strange about it?

Joanna was nervous—she hadn't realized quite *how* nervous. Jack could always do that to her . . . had been doing it to her for years now. Somehow it seemed there were only a few people in a lifetime who had that kind of power over you, and for her, Jack was one.

Taking a deep breath and letting it out slowly, Joanna rang the doorbell again. For a long moment she didn't hear anything. Then she heard the familiar sounds: a crash, probably Jack tripping over the corner of the coffee table on the way to the door, and fumbling and muttering on the other side as he struggled with the lock. Then, suddenly, the door opened.

Jack had obviously been sitting at his desk, working. His hair was rumpled, one piece standing straight up in the air the way it did when he'd been running his hands through it over and over again. His feet were bare, and his tie was half-unknotted and askew. He looked terrible—and more wonderful than anything she'd seen in weeks.

"Jack . . . I . . ." Now that the moment was actually here, she didn't know what to say. But it didn't really matter. Before the words could even take shape in her mouth, she found herself in Jack's arms, locked in an embrace of such trembling power and tender longing that it left her breathless.

"Joanna! I can't believe you're actually here. Do you know that I've been going crazy looking for you? I've called and called and couldn't get through to you, and then just this afternoon I went over and tried to get past that horrible woman who's been keeping you prisoner. I wanted to kill her. Joanna, did you know about my calls, that I've been trying to reach you?"

Joanna shook her head, not trusting herself to speak. Suddenly, with the front door closed behind her, and locked in Jack's arms, nothing mattered. Kay Chancellor and her silly clothes and wine lessons and selfish tantrums seemed to fade into the background as though they'd never been a part of her life. She hadn't felt so *right* in a long, long time, content to be exactly where she was, with the person she was with, at that moment in time.

"Oh, Jack, I've missed you so much. Ever since the other night, I haven't been able to think of anything but seeing you again." Jill felt reckless, happy, not caring about being careful, about saying too much.

Slowly, still holding her, Jack began to walk backward, bringing her out of the hall and into the living room. Nothing had changed very much, Joanna thought, registering the information without really taking it in. Jack was raining tiny kisses all over her face and neck, saying her name over and over.

Suddenly Joanna pulled away so that she could look into his eyes. "Jack, I have to leave Kay. Now. I couldn't stand it another minute. I think she really is crazy. Yes, I do feel like a prisoner there, I never knew how much until right now. She thinks she owns people. I heard her talking to Brock today like

138

he was some delivery boy she'd never laid eyes on. She's a cold, scheming woman, and I've had enough. I don't know why I've been blind to her for so long. I guess because I needed comforting and attention, and she was there to give it."

"Come on, Joanna. Don't be too hard on yourself." Jack reached out to stroke her hair. "In her twisted way, she obviously cares a great deal about you. You were hurt, I'd treated you so badly, and it was natural to want that in your life. I just hope I can make it up to you. I want to, more than anything else in the world."

They moved toward each other slowly, and then Joanna was in his arms. It felt so wonderful to be near him again, to feel his strength, to breathe in his familiar smell. A wave of peace washed over her. Then his mouth came down on hers, probing, gentle, urgent, filled with the promise of more . . . much more.

As they kissed, Joanna's mind floated off in a whirl of thoughts and feelings. Maybe Jack's marriage to Peggy had never even happened—had never even existed. Maybe it was all in her imagination, and she'd never been out of Jack's arms for even a day, a minute . . .

For a moment, she felt herself drowning in a warm bath of long-forgotten sensation. Then, suddenly, she had a flash of remembering. *But he left me*, whispered a small voice, almost too tiny to be heard over the rushing and pounding of her blood. *But he left me.*

In one swift motion, Jack scooped her off her feet and, his lips still on hers, carried her toward the bedroom.

Chapter Ten

A Tender Prize

Jill couldn't believe it. The scene she'd fantasized about for weeks now was actually going to happen —tonight. She felt her stomach flip-flop pleasantly as she slid lower in the bathtub and let out a deep sigh. She was a lucky woman.

Fate was such a strange thing. If her father had never been sick, never gone into the hospital just when he did, she would probably never have met David Mallory. They came from different parts of town and moved in different circles of Genoa City —there was no logical reason for them ever to have met, unless they'd bumped into each other by chance.

It gave Jill a sense of panic to imagine never having met David. How would she be feeling now? Instead of this nervous excitment, a newly aroused interest in life where everything suddenly looked brighter, as though the world had suddenly been brought into sharp focus for the very first time—she would be living in a world of grays. Her father dead, her mother off in her own world somewhere, even her brothers, concerned though they were, involved with their own lives. She would feel totally and utterly alone. Instead, she felt happy, excited, filled with an unfamiliar energy.

Turning around to look at the dainty bathroom clock that sat on her little vanity, Jill swore softly and stood up in the tub. She'd been so unaware of herself these days—visiting the hospital, keeping vigil first by her father's side, then David's—that it was as if she'd become unfamiliar with her own body. Now she looked at herself appraisingly in the long mirror on the bathroom wall, turning to get the full effect.

She was still in pretty good shape, even though she'd been neglecting her exercises. But that would change; all that would change. David had said something about enjoying tennis. Suddenly her mind was off again, painting one of the pictures she'd become so good at creating, filling in the blank spaces with color, shadow and shape.

There they were, after the last set of tennis, walking off the court together hand in hand. She imagined the way David would look after a vigorous game of tennis, his muscular arms and chest covered in a fine film of sweat, his tanned legs lean and hard in his white shorts. They would go over to one of the little tables at the club and order a cool drink, then sit there together, just watching people, happy in each other's company. Then . . .

Jill shook herself. What was wrong with her? The real thing, the flesh-and-blood guy, was coming over to dinner in just over an hour, and she was standing here with no clothes on, daydreaming about an afternoon at the tennis club.

Toweling her hair dry, she walked into her bedroom and opened her closet, standing back to survey her wardrobe. She wanted to choose just the right thing. In her fantasies, she'd worn the black silk kimono, but now that the evening had arrived, it didn't seem quite right. There was something too somber, too seriously seductive about it. No. She cocked her head to one side and ran a hand over the clothes that hung on padded silk and wooden hangers, as though her hand might stop suddenly, of its own accord, at just the right choice.

After thinking a moment more, she went over to her bureau and pulled out a pair of nicely fitting oatmeal linen slacks and a soft cream jersey top. Then she dried her hair, brushed it until it shone and applied a little blush, mascara and some light lipstick. Face it. She wasn't a vamp—she'd never be a vamp —and that was obviously not the woman David Mallory had been attracted to.

Daubing a little perfume on her wrists and behind her ears, Jill stepped back to look at herself, satisfied. Even she could see there was something soft and open about her lately, accessible. She didn't *feel* tight inside. It was as though some tightly closed flower had gently begun to open up inside her, one soft petal at a time, until she felt . . . well, "blooming" was probably the best word she could think of.

It scared her to think that David had the power to make her feel that way. Because that meant he also had the power to take that feeling away. But she was willing to do everything she could to keep him in her life. Even if she had to wait; even if it took some time.

In the past, Jill had always been the one to be pursued. So many of her relationships had been a case of fighting off a man's attentions until she just didn't—couldn't—fight anymore. There had always been, somewhere, the feeling of losing a major battle —even if she had felt passion and warmth, too, the overwhelming sensation was one of simply giving in.

This was so different. She wanted this, wanted it with all her heart. Instead of being pursued, looking behind her shoulder constantly to see if someone was closing the gap, she was now stepping forward, reaching out with open arms to embrace whatever the future might hold.

Forty-five more minutes. Jill did a quick tour of the apartment, knowing without needing to look that everything was sparkling. After she'd dropped David off in downtown Genoa City yesterday, she'd come straight home and started to clean and polish, knowing that he was coming tonight. The activity had also kept her mind occupied.

Where had David been going? Why had he seemed so vague about where he lived? Why hadn't he wanted her to drop him off at his home? He had to be feeling pretty weak, after having had little or no exercise in over a month. But, as usual, he'd gently evaded her tentative questions.

"I have some things to take care of downtown. I'll be fine. Don't worry about me. I've been out of circulation for a long time." His voice had been teasing. "And I have a lot of catching up to do. Look, I'll be seeing you tomorrow night like we planned, okay?" He'd put his hand under her chin and raised her head so that he was looking straight into her eyes. "You go home and get some rest. You've been putting in too many hours beside a hospital bed for someone so young and beautiful."

Gently he'd kissed her on her lips and on the tip of her nose, then opened the car door. "Tomorrow." He'd searched her face, then gotten out of the car and begun to walk toward the financial district, turning back once to wave.

Jill opened the fridge and began mentally going over the dinner she'd planned. A bottle of Dom Pérignon sat chilling in an antique silver ice bucket, a prize find from her flea marketing days. Two delicate fluted champagne glasses stood next to the bucket. She wanted to toast David's health. Even more than that, she wanted to toast their love. She just hoped he did, too.

They would start with the champagne and a delicate herbed cheese. She didn't want to have to keep running back and forth to the kitchen to cook, so she'd planned a menu that had been prepared ahead of time. Cream of watercress soup, followed by stuffed veal, which now sat warm and fragrant on top of the stove, ready for carving, along with rice pilaf and a salad. A bottle of expensive Chardonnay sat in the fridge in case the champagne ran out. And if they were up to it, a rich chocolate and Grand Marnier mousse was chilling in the fridge. Maybe they'd get around to dessert and coffee later. Jill shivered. She was as ready as she was ever going to be. She just wished the evening would hurry up and start.

When the doorbell rang, Jill stood for a moment in the hall, willing her heart to stop pounding. She thought David could probably hear it from where he stood, even with the door between them. Crossing and uncrossing her fingers, a gesture unconsciously recalled from childhood, she took a deep breath and opened the door.

"Hello, David."

He stood there looking even more handsome than she'd imagined. She was glad when she saw him that she'd chosen a simple, casual outfit rather than something long, trailing, black and seductive. David was wearing a pair of beautifully tailored gray slacks and a shirt that was open at the neck, with sleeves rolled up to reveal his strong forearms.

The difference between David Mallory in a hospital bed and David Mallory in her apartment was striking —in fact, almost breathtaking, she thought, and found that she was having trouble concentrating. He was so much bigger, more powerful. He seemed to fill her hallway with his shoulders, to look down at her from such a height.

"You're so big," she blurted out, then blushed, feeling foolish.

David laughed, his warm deep laugh that filled her with a rush of comforting warmth. This was the David she knew.

"Well, what do you expect? You've been looking down at me all these weeks. Now it's time for me to turn the tables—just for a little while, that is." His voice was teasing, gentle, filled with unspoken feeling.

"This is a nice place you have here." His hands deep in his pockets, he moved around the living room taking everything in, stopping to examine a print and a small piece of sculpture that stood on her desk.

"I made that," she said hesitantly, suddenly shy about revealing details about herself that had seemed to have no place in the hospital. "I used to be very interested in art. I don't do too much anymore."

David picked up the small stone figure and stroked it delicately, appreciating the lines with his fingers, the smoothness of the stone. "This is very beautiful. I'm impressed."

Suddenly he looked at her, eyebrows raised quizzically. The skin around his eyes was still bruised, but the whites were clearer now. He has such beautiful green eyes, she thought, really seeing them for the first time. They were a light green, almost like cat's eyes, with shots of amber running through them.

"Would you like some champagne?" Jill knew she must sound nervous, probably because she was. She'd felt so relaxed around David at the hospital, chattering away to him, sitting on the side of his bed, picking up his hand and playing with the fingers as though she'd known him forever. Now suddenly he was a stranger standing in her living room. She felt stiff and formal—and yet not.

"Before we have champagne, what I'd really like is a welcome-home kiss."

David held out his arms, and in a minute she was enfolded in his embrace. His breath tickled her ear as he murmured soft, unintelligible words. She closed her eyes, savoring the moment. And then he tilted her head back so that she was looking up at him.

"Jill," he said softly. "Jill, I've been waiting so long for this." His kiss was gentle, careful, but then became bolder, more searching. Jill's heart began to pound as wave after wave of sensation swept her body. She wanted his kiss to go on forever. When he finally did pull away, she kept her eyes closed for a moment, unwilling to let the moment end.

"How about that champagne," David said gently, taking her by the hand and leading her over to the table where the ice bucket and glasses were set out. "It seems like a million years since I've had a glass of champagne," he said jokingly, but his eyes remained serious, saying much, much more.

Dinner was delicious, and Jill found herself loosening up as the evening progressed. By the time

David rose to help her clear away the dishes, she was relaxed, talking easily, feeling as comfortable as she had back at the hospital.

It was only when the conversation moved to anything too personal that David seemed to retreat. During dinner, they had talked about her childhood, what it was like growing up with two brothers. But when she tried to turn the conversation to his family, David took her hand and turned it over so that he could kiss her palm. "I don't want to waste our time together talking about me and my family. We're not nearly as interesting as you are. Tell me more about growing up. I love hearing your stories."

"But David," Jill protested, pulling her hand away, "you never talk about yourself. Whenever I bring up the subject of your family or your work . . . or whether . . . there are any women in your life," she said with a rush, "you shut me out completely. You know practically my whole life history by now, and I don't even know where you live!"

Now she was angry—she could feel her blood pounding as she waited for him to answer. What if he just got up and walked away? What if one of the conditions to knowing—to loving—David Mallory was not knowing anything about his life, and not asking any questions? Well, she for one was not going to be able to put up with that kind of secrecy.

"Calm down, Jill," said David, refilling their wineglasses and then deliberately taking her hand back in his. "I don't think you understand. I'm not deliberately withholding anything from you. There's just not that much to tell. Let's see, I've told you that I own a contracting business. My family is from the east coast, New York, which is where I grew up, and I'm really not in touch with them much. I have one brother I haven't seen in five or six years. And as for the women in my life, I've already told you. There have been women, sure, but there's no one special right now. Okay? Do you believe me?"

David's tone was gentle, almost mocking. Jill looked up into his eyes. Why was it that she didn't quite believe him? Sure, she believed that what he had just told her was the truth. But what had he *really* told her?

Obviously, David was a very private man, a loner of sorts, and he didn't like telling his personal business to anyone. But she wasn't just anyone. And she couldn't help but feel that no matter how hard she tried to read between the lines, she wasn't going to be able to dredge up any more information from David's easy, soothing statements.

But what did she want? What was she looking for? She didn't want confessions and stories just for their own sake. She wanted to *know* this man, really know him. And how was she supposed to do that when his life was a blank wall?

"As for where I live," David continued, "before I went into the hospital so suddenly, I was in the process of looking for a house in Genoa City. That was all put on hold, obviously, and it's one of the first things I have to take care of. Most of my stuff is in storage—a few things are still back in New York City—because I was living in an apartment. You know, my contracting business here is pretty new. I used to be based in New York, and then decided to try my luck here."

"But what made you decide on Genoa City?" Jill hated the plaintive, distrusting tone she heard in her own voice, but she couldn't help it.

"You don't think everyone in New York City has

heard of Genoa City?" he asked teasingly. "No, seriously, my partner is from around this area. He was a transplanted midwesterner on the east coast, so I decided it was time to take my turn and come out here. We came to Genoa City less than a year ago to set up business. I've been staying with him. And so far I like it here just fine."

His green eyes held hers, and she felt a smile tug at the corners of her mouth. "I'm sorry, David. I must seem like the nosiest person on earth. It's just that I feel like I know you so well in some ways, and then I suddenly ask myself what I really know about you, and I have to say, 'Nothing.' I guess in my experience those two things don't add up. To feel close to someone, intimate, you have to understand who they are, where they came from, what makes them tick. With you, I feel like it's the other way around. Do you understand what I mean?" Her voice was pleading, hesitant. She had been so determined to make this a wonderful, perfect evening, and here she had practically ruined it with her prying.

"Of course I know what you mean," David said soothingly, drawing her to the sofa in front of the bay window that looked out over the city. "But what I want to do now is sit with a very beautiful lady and look out at her beautiful city after a very beautiful dinner. Does that meet your requirements?"

Jumping up suddenly, Jill went over to the oak sideboard in the dining room and, after rummaging around for a minute, came back triumphantly bearing a bottle of cognac. "Ta-*da!* I knew I had some of this stuff somewhere. Would you like some?"

Jill wasn't used to drinking, and they'd already consumed the bottle of champagne and the Chardonnay. She felt a little giddy, light-headed, her mood soaring high, then faltering, then rising again. She felt reckless, as if she were on a roller coaster ride and had no desire—no intention—of stopping.

"Sure, why not. This is supposed to be a celebration, isn't it?"

Jill found two balloon brandy snifters in the cupboard and walked over in her bare feet to where David had settled himself comfortably on the sofa. She sat down next to him, unconsciously snuggling up close, forgetting that just moments before she had accused him of being a stranger.

As they buried their noses in the brandy, sniffing appreciatively, Jill sighed in contentment, pushing her doubts aside for the moment.

"Oh, David. It's so incredible to have you here. I've dreamed often of tonight," she confessed shyly, taking little sips of brandy to cover her confusion. "I've dreamed that it would be like this, and now I'm not sure that it's really happening—or whether I'm still dreaming. Tell me I'm not still dreaming. . . ."

David set his snifter carefully on the coffee table and reached over to take her glass from her hand and set it down next to his. Then he took her by the shoulders and brought her down so that her head was resting against his chest. She could feel the rhythmic thud of his heartbeat, could smell the fresh, crisp scent of his shirt mixed with the faint tang of his after-shave. She closed her eyes, savoring the moment, almost unable to hear his words because she was so overwhelmed with different sensations.

"Jill, you've become very important to me these last few weeks. More important than I can say. I hope you understand that. If I seem a little distant at times, I'm sorry. Please bear with me. There are a few things

I have to sort out in my life, that I have to take care of.
But I want you to trust me. I want that more than
anything in the world."

His arm tightened around her shoulders, massaging them gently. His breath was hot, fragrant with
brandy, as he moved from her ear, down her neck,
tracing warm, teasing circles with his tongue. By the
time he reached her mouth, Jill felt weak with longing.

"David, I . . . I . . ."

"Don't say anything. You don't have to say anything."

His mouth came down on hers again, and she
arched against him, shutting out the world, shutting
out her thoughts.

The call from the hospital came at 5:05 that morning.
Jennifer Brooks's vital signs were failing, her pulse
was erratic and weak: Stuart should plan to gather his
family together and come to the hospital as soon as
possible. It looked like the end.

Stuart felt a strange calm steal over him. He
dressed quickly and efficiently, not stopping to shower or shave. Now that the moment he had awaited
—had dreaded—for so long was finally here, he
hardly felt anything.

Maybe that was one of the blessings of nature, he
thought, of being close to the animals. Our systems
simply shift to automatic pilot, shutting out all
thought, all feeling. That would come later, he knew.
Now it was simply survival, getting through the next
hours and days.

At least there would soon be peace for Jennifer.
During all this time, the knowledge of her pain had

haunted him. To know that she was in agony almost any hour of the day or night was nearly more than he could bear. He'd come to understand why Liz had ended her own husband's life. Had Jennifer asked him to, he would have gladly taken the risk. But she hadn't.

She was—had been—so strong. Stuart stood by his dresser and picked up the photograph he had of Jennifer, framed in worn maroon leather. It had been sitting amidst tie clips and nail clippers and coins and odds and ends for over twenty years. Her head was thrown back in one of the big, open laughs that he so loved, and her blond hair was blowing back into her face. If his memory still served him, the photograph had been taken aboard a ferry going to Nova Scotia on one of their first vacations together, before any of the girls were born.

For a moment he was there again, feeling the salt spray, the smell of her sun-warmed hair and skin, the way she would lean over close to his ear and whisper, "I love you," at the strangest, most unexpected times. They'd had a good life together. It seemed unbelievable that it was over.

Suddenly Stuart felt bone weary. It was time to make some calls, locate the rest of the family and try to get them to come to the hospital.

Peggy. Stuart's heart sank, and he walked slowly over to the bed and sat down on the edge, resting his head between his hands. He just couldn't face it. How was he going to walk in there, look into that already tormented face and tell her that her mother was going to die within a few hours? What would it do to her?

But he had to tell her. Jennifer would understand if she wasn't there, but Peggy would never forgive him—he would never forgive himself—if he didn't give her the choice of saying good-bye to her mother.

Slowly, dragging one hand down his beard-roughened chin, he walked to Peggy's door, which was shut as always. He paused for a minute, then knocked softly.

"Peg, honey? Are you awake?" Hearing no answer, he quietly opened the door a crack and peeked in. Peggy was lying asleep, her bear clutched to her chest. Stuart felt a deep wrench inside him, and a sob rose in his chest.

What was life all about, anyway? Here was his beloved wife, dying, and his youngest daughter, a beautiful young woman, turned into a helpless child again.

Well, now obviously wasn't the time to try to figure out life's secrets. Squaring his shoulders, he walked into her bedroom. Sitting down gently on the edge of her bed so as not to startle her, he put his hand on her arm.

"Peggy, it's Daddy."

She woke with a start and sat up in bed with a sharp scream. Tiny beads of sweat had formed on her forehead and upper lip, and her hair was a wild tangle as though she'd been tossing and turning restlessly all night.

"Oh, Daddy . . ." She trailed off, then sank back into the pillows. "I was having this bad dream. . . ."

Stuart remembered when he and Jennifer had awakened in the night to little Peggy's shrill cries and come in together to comfort her after one of her childhood nightmares. Now here he was, all these years later, doing the same thing. Without Jennifer.

"Peggy, honey, listen to me. It's Mommy." He reached for both her hands and held them tightly, trying to get her to focus. He hated to add another nightmare—particularly this one—to the one she was already living. But he had no choice.

"The hospital just called, baby, and asked us to come and see her. Mom's worse, and they think she might not make it. Do you understand what I'm telling you?"

Tears welled up in Peggy's eyes and began to run down her face. She stared hard at her father, the vein in the middle of her forehead throbbing with the effort.

"Mommy . . ." she whispered.

"There isn't a lot of time, honey," said Stuart gently. "If you don't want to come to the hospital that's fine. Your mom will understand. If you'd like to come, I'll help you get dressed."

Suddenly Peggy turned over in bed and pulled the covers up past her chin, refusing to look at him.

Stuart stood by the bed for a moment, torn by indecision. Maybe if he stayed and coaxed her, she'd be able to break through the wall she'd erected around herself. But would that be for the best?

It took a lot of strength to say good-bye for the last time to your own mother.

Stroking her head and smoothing the blanket over her still form, he turned and left the room, closing the door softly behind him. This was one good-bye that he was going to have to make for her.

For a few minutes, she was there with him again —the Jennifer he knew and fell in love with. Wracked with pain, gaunt and pale, she was lying so still when he walked into her room that he thought he was too late. Standing by the bed, he reached out to touch her face, and suddenly her eyes opened.

"Stu-ar-t," she whispered, and the ghost of a smile passed over her face. For a second she opened her eyes wide, and with a pang he saw how beautiful and blue they still were, even through all that pain.

"Jenny, can you hear me?"

She nodded, barely moving her head, and the same shadowy smile passed over her face again.

"Peggy couldn't come. She's sick, but she's going to be fine. I'm taking care of her. She told me to tell you how much she loves you." The words caught in his throat, and he had to stop and grip the edge of the bed.

With a tiny movement, Jennifer gestured that she wanted to hold his hand. He took the long, frail hand and cupped it in both of his.

"The other kids are going to be here soon . . . Laurie, Leslie, Chris. I've told the nurse to send them in as soon as they get here."

Stuart trailed off, not sure what to say next. There was so much to say, and yet nothing to say. He could talk on for hours about their life together—how wonderful it had been, how much she had meant to him, how he was going to miss her terribly. But there wasn't time.

"Jennifer, I love you. I'll miss you."

She hadn't spoken yet, but now he could see her struggling to form words. He leaned closer, nodding encouragingly.

"St-u-ar-t." The whisper again, barely audible.

"Yes, Jenny, what is it, sweetheart?"

He waited, holding his breath as her eyelids flickered, but they opened again, this time with a new strength.

"The girls . . . take care of them. Peggy . . ."

Stuart nodded, waiting for her to continue.

"You . . . please . . . you must marry again." She clutched his hand with surprising strength as she saw him start to protest. "Promise me . . . that you won't be alone," she whispered, a smile raising the corners of her pinched mouth. "I don't want to think of you . . . all alone . . . in that old house. . . ."

Stuart smiled tenderly down at her and wiped the tears from the corners of her eyes. "Of course, Jenny. You always were the boss." He tried to say it lightly but found himself choking on the words.

"I . . . love you. I love you . . ." Her words trailed off and she closed her eyes, as though she'd used up the last of her strength.

"I love you, too," said Stuart, not knowing whether she could hear him anymore.

He stood beside her bed, holding her hand, looking down at the woman with whom he had spent the most wonderful years of his life, saying good-bye without words.

Thirty minutes later, Stuart felt her slip away. He kissed her good-bye for the last time, then went out to wait for their children.

Chapter Eleven

To Dream Again

The chapel was filled with flowers—Joanna had never seen so many in one room together. Obviously, Jennifer Brooks had been a very well-loved woman.

Joanna straightened the slim skirt of her silk suit and peeked out from under the brim of her hat to look next to her where Jack sat in the aisle seat of the pew. She wondered if he felt as strange as she did—almost sacrilegious or something. Well, just because people died didn't mean that other people stopped getting married, she thought, stifling a small giggle.

Nothing had ever felt more right to her than waking up in Jack Curtis's arms yesterday morning. So when he'd rolled over on one elbow, his hair rumpled from sleep and his eyes still half-closed and said, "Want to get married tomorrow?" she hadn't had to think twice. Well, that wasn't entirely true —maybe she'd thought about it for a second.

She knew it must seem insane for her to be eloping with Jack Curtis, her infamous ex-husband, the philanderer. But so what. It was her life to live as she pleased. The way she looked at it, Jack had had a lot of growing up to do, and he'd simply gone and done it when she wasn't around.

Maybe they *were* rushing into things too fast, but what good ever came of waiting? And the look on Kay Chancellor's face when she saw her ring would make it worthwhile, even if the marriage only lasted a week, Joanna thought triumphantly.

It was unfortunate that the short wedding ceremony at city hall had had to be on the same day as Jennifer Brooks's funeral, but that was just the way things had happened. Who could plan on births, deaths or marriages—well, at least *her* marriages.

Joanna reached over and squeezed Jack's hand. She hoped he was as happy as she was right now. After the funeral, they were planning to hop in the car and just take off, like old times, and wherever the car landed them—that would be their honeymoon spot.

The organ music began to play softly as the chapel started to fill. Joanna tried not to crane her neck, but it was hard to resist turning around and watching everyone as they filed in. Weddings and funerals had always seemed so much alike to her. Well, obviously one was a lot sadder, but other than that, what was the difference?

She noticed Stuart Brooks and two of his daughters, Leslie and Laurie, standing at the back door of the church, greeting people. Stuart looked very tall and handsome in a dark suit. Poor man, she thought. However, the end had to be a relief after such an ordeal.

The Fosters came in next. Snapper supported a rather tired looking Chris, who joined her father at the door. Greg escorted his mother. Joanna watched as Liz stopped and shook herself free of her son so that she could speak to Stuart. She had to stand almost on tiptoe to get close enough, Joanna observed, suppressing a smile.

She'd heard that Liz hadn't been doing so well since her husband died—in fact, had not really been quite right in the head for a while. But she looked wonderful now. In fact, she looked downright stunning, dressed in an elegant black dress with a small black veiled hat. They made a nice couple, Liz and Stuart, thought Joanna, then she shook herself. Hey, give the pair a little time. Just because *some* people don't wait.

David and Jill were behind Liz, Jill hovering protectively over her mother, obviously torn between her and the gorgeous man she was with. Joanna had heard rumors about this guy—he owned some kind of construction business, and he'd been in the hospital and got Bill Foster's eyes, something like that.

There was also talk about some shady dealings he'd left behind him on the east coast. But then, that was Kay Chancellor talking, and if there was the slightest opportunity to ruin a nice romance, she'd be standing there, first in line. Shady dealings or no, it looked as if it didn't matter a bit to Jill. And besides, who cared what a guy did if he was that good-looking? In all her gossiping, Kay had conveniently neglected to mention how incredibly handsome he was. Instinctively, Joanna preened, and then gave herself a mental slap. Down, girl. You're a happily married woman—again.

She shivered, thinking about the night that still lay ahead. She'd packed a nightgown to end all nightgowns in her overnight bag. What did it matter that Kay had given it to her? Who wanted to split hairs when you were talking about a black silk Christian Dior negligee cut to the waist?

If she knew her ex-ex-husband, he wouldn't worry about it for a second.

Liz Foster settled herself in the pew next to the aisle and breathed a sigh of relief. She'd felt such a sense of urgency about coming to the funeral today, about seeing Stuart and making sure he was all right. It was strange to be at another funeral so soon after Bill's, especially when that one remained such a surreal and hazy memory for her—hardly even a memory at all.

It might sound crazy, and a lot of people wouldn't understand, but because she'd been so unable to experience Bill's death at the time, to feel anything at his funeral, it was almost as though this were Bill's funeral, too. Not that she was taking anything at all away from Jennifer Brooks. But privately, just to herself, this was a funeral for both of them.

Maybe it was because she'd been feeling so close to Stuart ever since Bill's death. Stuart had been so strong for her, so *there*, that she'd wanted to rush to him the moment she'd heard Jennifer had finally gone. But he had his family, his daughters, and it hadn't seemed quite right.

She only hoped that he understood how much she felt for him, how much she shared in his grief and his feelings of loss. She was pretty sure he did know. They were like that together, sharing something that seemed almost like telepathy. You didn't have to speak—you just knew.

Following the afternoon that Stuart had brought her back—she didn't know how else to describe it—she had thought a great deal about him. Maybe it seemed wrong or inappropriate to be thinking about

Stuart as a man at his own wife's funeral, but she didn't think so.

Liz had loved Jennifer as a friend and respected the Brooks's marriage, despite its difficulties. After all, what family didn't have its ups and downs? It was probably just for that reason—the fact that they'd had such a basically good marriage in so many ways—that Liz was so drawn to Stuart. He was a truly good man in a world where those qualities were rare.

Liz wanted to be a friend to Stuart, a good friend. She wanted to help him through this time, as he'd helped her. She looked toward the back of the chapel where he stood in the doorway greeting the last few stragglers. He looked tired, so, so tired. She knew what that kind of tired felt like—the kind where you didn't think you'd ever be able to lift your head again, let alone take a step. Well, with Stuart's help, she'd learned that that kind of feeling didn't have to last forever.

She watched as he bent to greet a small child who had just come in with her mother. He was a kind man, someone who would step out of his way to help someone. He had helped her, more than he could ever know.

Turning back to face the altar, she folded her hands and said a small prayer, for Bill, for Jennifer, for Stuart and for herself.

It was the strangest feeling, Jill thought, but when she stood with David, behind her mother, watching her talk to Stuart Brooks, she'd actually felt jealous. There was something about the power, the bond, that seemed to connect those two. She wasn't talking about sex. More than anything, they seemed to love each other as friends, to share something, some knowledge, something so big that it excluded everyone else.

Jill shook herself. Obviously she wasn't jealous just because the two of them shared the common bond of death in their lives. That would be crazy. But this was different: there was something more.

Maybe it was because Jill had been feeling how strangely tenuous a connection love could be. She was pretty sure she loved David, and yet that wonderful, powerful feeling seemed attached only to the finest thread of truth or reality.

She wanted a bond that was deep and powerful in her life, built on years of trust and caring. You didn't build that overnight. But would she ever be able to build that with a man who was incapable of opening himself up to her?

And, she thought, catching sight of Kay Chancellor sitting in the back of the chapel, would her love endure a threat that was much more immediate, much closer to home—the divisive power of gossip?

She'd heard the rumor about David Mallory just yesterday from a friend of Kay Chancellor's who happened to stop by on some pretext and casually dropped the news. It infuriated Jill that she would stoop so low as to listen to rumors—particularly about David—but she was so hungry for information about him that it was hard to ignore anything that came her way.

Did Jill know, the woman had said, lowering her voice conspiratorially, that this David Mallory had had to leave the east coast because he'd been involved in some pay-off scandal in the construction industry? He had come out here to Genoa City to try and make a new name for himself, but just look what he'd left behind. . . .

Her voice had droned on and on, and Jill had found herself tuning it out. It was ironic, but suddenly, because of having been offered the last piece of the puzzle by this prying old busybody, the picture was finally beginning to take shape.

Of course David would be reluctant to talk about anything that had to do with where he came from, if he'd left a scandal of some sort behind. Whether it was his job, his family or his roots—it didn't matter. No wonder she'd felt as if there were a wall between them—there had been. He probably wasn't lying to her, but obviously he was withholding some of the truth—a very important part of the truth.

She loved David, and she wasn't going to turn away from him because of some mistake in his past. Whatever had happened, whatever he'd been involved in, she wanted to hear it from him.

Jill glanced over at David now, mentally caressing his profile. She didn't care if there was a blotch on his past. Everyone made mistakes. She'd certainly made more than her fair share. If he could forgive her her errors, she would certainly do the same for him.

David could see again. If miracles like that could happen, she wasn't about to let something as petty as a few nasty rumors ruin what they had together. Anyway, the gossip would die down. It always did.

But so could love if it wasn't treated with care.

Kay Chancellor sat near the back of the church. It had always made her extremely uncomfortable to sit too near the front anywhere—at the theater or at the movies—but particularly in church. Maybe it was because from the back you had a much better grasp of what was going on—who came late, left early, fell asleep or whispered during the sermon.

She had invited her son to accompany her to the

funeral, but Brock didn't seem to be on speaking terms with her. Now that Joanna had flown the coop, so to speak, maybe Brock would forgive her. Had she said unforgivable things that day? Probably. She'd been pretty insensitive in her time, and even her own son wasn't divinely protected from her sharp tongue.

She loved Brock, but he made her so impatient. He was too concerned with other people's lives, too wrapped up in solving other people's problems, when he needed to pay attention to his own. That was one trait he hadn't gotten from her.

Well, maybe Joanna had been an exception.

What was it about Joanna? From her vantage point in the back, Kay watched as Joanna leaned over to whisper in Jack's ear. She was wearing such a ridiculous little hat, she thought, and acting as though he were the only man on earth. Kay had tried to teach her some taste. Obviously in some areas she had failed miserably. What did she care about that air-brained tramp, anyway? Sometimes Kay puzzled even herself.

When Joanna hadn't come back by dinnertime after going to the pool that afternoon, Kay had grown worried. But when she'd called the club, and the manager had said she'd left in the late afternoon, Kay had begun to do a little addition. Their fight, plus Jack's surprise visit, plus Joanna's sudden little burst of independence—it all added up to Joanna running crying to Jack. . . .

Joanna didn't show up at all that evening, and by ten P.M. Kay was seething. She marched right up to Joanna's room in a kind of concentrated fury and flung all her clothes onto the floor, a ridiculous, childish gesture that accomplished absolutely nothing, except that it made her feel a hundred percent better. Then she went downstairs, poured herself a very dry martini and enjoyed every last drop of it. After that she had another one. And after that, she stopped—a seemingly impossible feat in everyone else's estimation of her—and went up to bed, pleasantly drunk and quite pleased with herself.

But while she was drinking her martinis, she figured something out. All the time Joanna was with her, she hadn't had one drink. Maybe Joanna had been her substitute for alcohol. Here was this pathetic, malleable creature with no taste or sophistication who simply needed someone to come along and take an interest in her. And what better person than a reformed drunk with more money than she knew what to do with? Dressing Joanna, feeding Joanna and teaching Joanna how to use a fish fork were like a three-martini high: power, control, with the occasional headache in the morning to endure.

What was infatuation, anyway? Kay mused. Did it really have anything to do with another person, or was it more self-centered? Poor Joanna. She was probably dying to wave that sad little ring in her face and have her throw a fit. Well, it wasn't going to happen. Kay just didn't care anymore. Joanna would have to go ahead and enjoy her mistake all by herself. . . .

When Brock arrived at the chapel it was close to full. He pulled into the parking lot, noticing that his mother's car was first in line. You've done it again, Mother dear, he thought bitterly. First in line at the funeral. Funerals, relationships—Kay Chancellor tried her best to upstage everything.

He sat for a minute, feeling the car engine tick, reluctant to go in. He'd wanted to come to Jennifer's funeral, and he wasn't going to let his mother or Joanna get in his way. He just didn't want to have to face either of them right now. He'd planned on arriving late like this, so that he could just slip quietly into a back pew and then leave when it was over, hopefully unnoticed. His mother had eyes in the back of her head, he knew, but maybe this time he'd get lucky.

Even Kay couldn't have planned it better, he thought gleefully when he slipped into the very last pew at the back. The organ music was beginning to fade away, and he looked around quickly. The service would be starting any minute.

The perfume from the flowers was cloying, almost nauseating. He noticed his mother sitting a few rows ahead, practically in front of him. Her shoulders were stiff and set, and she had what he called her "proud look" on. It said, Don't touch me, don't talk to me, because I'm better than you. It was an attitude toward life that had made her a very unhappy woman.

Suddenly there was a rustling in the chapel, just as the minister rose to begin the service. Brock turned around, along with a few others, to see who was arriving so late. A near audible gasp rippled through the chapel as Peggy Brooks walked slowly down the aisle toward the front as though in a trance.

There weren't too many surprises or secrets that escaped watchful eyes in Genoa City, and Brock knew that Peggy's unstable mental state was already the subject of gossip. No one had expected her to be able to make it to her mother's funeral—least of all her own father.

Well, things can look very different suddenly, sometimes at the strangest moments, thought Brock, looking at the back of his mother's head. Good old

Peggy, he thought. Maybe she just woke up this morning and had the strength to go through with this. And that was the only thing anyone could trust—how you felt *today*. He bent his head and in a soft voice began to join in the prayer.

Stuart Brooks was stunned to see his youngest daughter walking down the aisle, ghostly pale in a black dress, her eyes never leaving his face. It was as though she needed to find a compass point in order to navigate her way.

The tears that had been threatening to spill over all morning now fell unheeded down his cheeks. It must have cost her more than anyone could know to come here today, with all of Genoa City to watch and whisper.

When Stuart had returned home following Jennifer's death two mornings ago, he'd found the house in shambles, as though in his absence a tornado had ripped through each room, tossing lamps on the floor, scattering vases and pictures every which way. . . .

His first thought was for Peggy. The house must have been burgled while he was away, and she was lying up there, helpless. What else could have happened? Please, God, he prayed as he raced up the stairs two at a time. Please, God, not again. Please don't let it have happened to Peggy again. Don't let her be hurt. She won't be able to handle it this time; she's just not strong enough.

Peggy wasn't in her room. Frantic, he raced into every room upstairs until he came to their bedroom —his bedroom, now. He found Peggy sitting on the floor sobbing, holding the picture of Jennifer that he'd been looking at only hours before. She was cradling it in her arms, then pressing it to her chest, moaning and rocking as though she'd never stop.

Stuart had thought that nothing more could get to him now. He'd felt as though all the feeling, all the emotion, had been wrung from him. He was simply a robot, going through the motions. But the sight of his youngest daughter sitting in her old oversize high school T-shirt mourning her lost mother brought everything back.

"Peggy, sweetheart!" He rushed over to her, not stopping to think about what was best, not trying this time to figure out the most psychologically correct way to reach Peggy. He reacted like a father, like a man who had just lost his wife, like the wounded animal he was. All he wanted was to crawl next to the closest living thing and seek comfort.

He got down beside her on the floor and gathered her, picture and all, into his arms. With his arms around her, he joined her in a rocking rhythm, emitting small, soothing sounds in counterpoint to her keening cries of grief and loss. He sat there holding her until the morning sun rose high enough to dapple the faded Oriental rug on the bedroom floor.

Eventually Peggy fell into a deep, exhausted sleep in his arms. He eased her onto the floor and rose, stiff, to take a pillow and a blanket from the bed. He placed the pillow under her head, still damp from her frenzy of rage, and covered her in the blanket. Then he left the bedroom door open, not wanting her to wake up and feel frightened.

He walked out of the room and went slowly down the stairs, feeling more tired than he'd ever felt in his life, but strangely at peace. It was as though Peggy's strange, frantic destruction of the house had released some of the demons that had been trapped inside her. The rape, then the failure of her marriage, and now her mother's death. Maybe Jennifer's dying, leaving her that way, had just been too much, and she'd been forced to vent some of that anger and disappointment or explode.

Stuart didn't pretend to understand fully what had happened to his daughter. But it felt to him, even as he started restoring order to the house, as if Peggy had chosen the time of her mother's death to have her own private exorcism. It was her way of protesting her mother's death, of saying, No I don't want this, just as I didn't want to be raped and I didn't want my marriage to fail.

At least she had come out of her room. He knew how to deal with anger, with rage, with *action*. Before, he had been helpless. Now he could help Peggy. She had finally called out, reached out, in whatever way she could. And, thank God, he could say, I'm still here, and I won't leave you.

But her recovery wasn't going to be immediate. When she awoke, he managed to persuade her to come downstairs and eat a bowl of soup and some crackers. She didn't ask about her mother, but he knew that would come later. He told her that the funeral was the next day, but he never thought she would come. Later, not yet, he was going to suggest that she see Dr. Vaughan. But he would give her time. . . .

Now he stretched out a hand to her, to help her the last few feet of her long walk down the aisle, and pulled her into the pew next to him.

"Thank you for coming, Peggy," he whispered, kissing her cheek. "Thank you for being here with us, honey."

She didn't look at him, but as they bowed their heads in prayer, she slipped her hand into his.

Joanna brushed away the tears from under her veil and followed the other mourners who had begun to walk away from the fresh mound of earth toward the row of gleaming black limousines parked near the gravesite.

Jack had walked on ahead to find out which car they were to return in. He looked so handsome in his dark suit, his hair shining in the sun, that for a moment Joanna felt a tug of pure happiness.

She breathed in deeply, almost tasting the fresh, blossom-scented air, then let it out shakily. It had been a beautiful service. She felt a strange mixture of feelings—sadness for Jennifer and the Brooks family, and a happy, grateful thankfulness tinged with something like fear for herself, for her good fortune, for the surprising turn her life had so suddenly taken.

Peggy Brooks had looked so lost, so brave, standing next to her father by the grave that it had just about broken her heart. Joanna had been a little worried about appearing at the funeral with Jack, wondering if Peggy would be there and if it would add to her pain to see them together. But Peggy seemed completely oblivious to everyone but her father.

Joanna had gone up to her after the service in the chapel and pressed her hand, murmuring a few comforting words. Peggy had responded politely, but distantly, as she did to everyone, as though she didn't quite know who it was behind each concerned handshake or kiss.

Maybe that's what happened when you lost someone you loved, thought Joanna. You retreated for a while, like a wounded animal, until you were ready to face the world again. Maybe that's what she'd been doing with Kay. Obviously losing your mother was different from losing a husband, but Joanna thought she knew what suffering and loss were all about. She'd needed to escape, too, to hide herself in some comfortable little cave and just be taken care of until she was ready to come out again. She thought she could understand how Peggy was feeling.

Joanna looked up from her musings to see Kay Chancellor headed her way. Her heart sank. Kay looked perfectly put together, as usual, in a beautifully cut black suit that Joanna had never seen before. There were a lot of things about Kay that she'd never seen before, she thought grimly, steeling herself for a confrontation.

"Kay," she said coolly, stopping and then moving away from the other mourners. She had no idea how Kay had taken her desertion and waited to see how the battle lines would be drawn. "You look lovely. That's a beautiful suit."

"Why, thank you, Joanna." Kay's voice dripped sarcasm. "You know how much your compliments mean to me. You have such good taste."

This was going to be worse than she had anticipated, Joanna thought. It didn't seem quite right to have a knock-down-drag-out fight with Kay Chancellor, not ten yards away from Jennifer Brooks's grave, but then Kay had never been big on decorum or propriety—or waiting.

"Well, you ought to know—you gave it to me," replied Joanna sarcastically. Then she sighed. "Kay, can't this wait? I don't think this is quite the time or the place to talk."

"Well, since you obviously can't bear to be away

from your beloved new husband for a second," Kay said, looking pointedly at her new ring, then over to where Jack waited, "now seems as good a time as any to me. Let's start with why the hell you walked out on me without so much as a phone call. Didn't your mother teach you good manners?"

Joanna felt helpless tears well up in her eyes. She was no match for Kay's sharp tongue. "Kay," she began pleadingly, "I'm sorry. I just needed to get away. I don't know, it happened suddenly, and I couldn't think of doing it any other way. I thought you'd be angry, and I guess I was scared to tell you. . . ." Joanna trailed off, hating the apologetic tone she heard in her voice.

"I guess I should have expected you to leave that way. When it comes to Jack Curtis, you don't have any willpower at all, do you?"

"Kay, that's not fair. You know I love him. I've never stopped loving him. I know you don't approve of what he did, but you don't have to be so cruel. He made a mistake, that's all. So do lots of people. I love him."

"What about the trip to Hawaii?" The question was cold, flat.

Joanna paused, not sure what to say. She played with the strap of her bag, searching for the right words. "No, I . . . I guess I won't be going with you to Hawaii. I'm sorry," she said simply, not wanting to lie.

"I don't know what makes you think you can do this. Walk out on me and then throw yourself on Jack. What makes you think he really wants you this time? What makes you think he won't string you along for a little while and then dump you again?"

Kay's voice was rising, and Joanna looked over

uneasily to where Jack was waiting for her, signaling her to join him.

"You know, I'm drinking again, Joanna. Since you left, I've been drinking every night." Kay's voice continued to rise, and Joanna wondered if she'd already had a few this morning.

Suddenly she felt a rush of anger. Who did this woman think she was, anyway, criticizing her, mocking her decisions, and then turning around and blaming her for something she'd had nothing to do with.

"Kay, you may not like Jack or think that I've made the right decision," Joanna said coldly. "The way I left may not have been the best, and I'm sorry. But I will *not* take responsibility for your drinking. If you want to ruin your life and drink yourself to death, go ahead. I'm not going to stop you. You don't need my permission or anyone else's. I know what self-destructive behavior is all about. Believe me, I know. And I refuse to feel guilty for something that has nothing to do with me. Thank you for being so generous to me, Kay. But I don't owe you a damn thing."

Turning on her heel, she walked away, leaving Kay standing there. Joanna walked quickly, then broke into a run, wobbling on her high-heeled pumps as they caught in the grass, a sob catching in her throat. Kay Chancellor could do as she damn well pleased. Right now, Joanna was going to begin a honeymoon.

Chapter Twelve

Endings and Beginnings

Brock watched as his mother stood at the airport check-in desk, first complaining to the woman behind the counter about her seat designation, then admonishing the luggage handler who was slinging her bags onto the conveyer belt to take extra care. Some things simply never changed, thought Brock fondly.

It seemed strange that his feelings toward his mother could have changed so drastically in such a short time.

He'd walked up to his mother following Jennifer's burial, just moments after Joanna had stormed off. Kay had been standing there, not moving, looking for once as though she had no idea what to do with herself. Brock had felt sorry for her, an emotion he had rarely, if ever, experienced toward his cold, sharp-tongued mother. She'd looked so rejected that Brock's heart had gone out to her. . . .

"Mom, are you all right?" He took her arm.

"Oh, Brock. Hi. Yes, I'm all right."

She looked around, bewildered, as though she didn't quite know where she was.

"Would you like me to drive you home?"

"Yes, oh, yes that would be nice," she said vaguely. He wasn't quite sure she'd even heard his question. "But first, why don't we go and visit Phillip's grave."

Brock was so stunned by her sudden suggestion that he gasped. The death of her husband—Brock's father—was something they had never discussed. The subject was strictly off limits, and whenever Brock had tried to bring it up in the past, she had turned on him viciously. The horrible car accident that had caused his death was something, she said, that she never wanted to think about again as long as she lived.

All Brock really knew, would ever really know, about the accident was that his mother had been driving—and that only she had survived the terrible fall over the cliff.

But there had been lots of rumors. Kay was drinking heavily at the time, and her husband was threatening to divorce her and marry a younger woman. Knowing his mother, with her fits of blind, jealous rage and her scheming, vindictive streak, Brock could only suspect what might have happened. He didn't think he really wanted to know, for sure, whether his mother had been responsible for his father's death.

Maybe he had loved his father more because he was kind and gentle. But he still loved his mother. And she was all he had left.

Occasionally Brock had gone to visit his father's grave by himself. He never knew whether Kay went or not but suspected that she had never set foot anywhere nearby. Now, it turned out that he was wrong. They were close enough to walk on foot to the grave, where a bouquet of flowers, not quite wilted, was propped against the smooth pink granite stone.

Brock watched as his mother stooped and ran a hand over the gravestone, spelling out Phillip's name with her fingers. The unselfconscious gesture made him blink back tears. She still loves him, Brock thought suddenly, shocked at the realization. I thought she hated him . . . but somewhere, she still loves him.

He stooped down beside her and reached over to pinch the dead blossoms off the bouquet, wondering who had brought the flowers. Maybe his mother had.

"Your father was a good man, Brock. I didn't treat him very well." It was a flat statement, without judgment or apology.

Brock held his breath, waiting for her to continue.

"It was my fault that he fell in love with someone else. I drove him to it. I miss him. You may find that hard to believe, but I do."

Brock stood, hearing the note of finality in her voice, and reached down to help her get up. For a moment she stood close to him, looking up into his face.

"I'm sorry about Joanna, Brock. I don't know if you heard any of our conversation, but she's going. She's already gone, actually," she said with a derisive laugh. "She won't be staying with me anymore. You're probably relieved to hear that," she added dryly.

She put her arm in his, and they turned and began slowly walking back over to the car.

"Maybe I will take that trip to Hawaii," she said. "Alone. I don't suppose you'd like to come with me." It was more a statement than a question, which saved him from having to respond.

"No, maybe it will do me good to get away by myself," she continued after a moment. "I'll get some sun and relax. Besides, they make great drinks over there, and there are lots of incredibly handsome men around. Yes, I think maybe I'll do just that. . . ."

Now Brock walked with his mother to the departing gate. She was one of the last passengers to have checked in, and everyone else had already boarded. That was Kay Chancellor for you—she'd keep them all waiting if she had a mind to.

Just outside the boarding gate Kay turned, ticket in hand, to face him. Brock had a sudden vision of her arrival in Hawaii, of the imperious way she would bend her head to receive the proffered lei or simply wave it away with a dismissive gesture, looking disdainfully around at the lush surroundings as though to say, "Not bad, for an island."

She was quite an amazing woman, his mother.

"Good-bye, Brock. Take care of yourself," Kay said briskly, pressing her cheek to his and kissing the air beside his ear.

She pulled back and they stared at each other for a moment. Then she turned and started down the ramp into the plane. But when she was about half-way down the ramp, she stopped in her tracks and turned suddenly, as though she'd forgotten something.

"You know," she said in a loud voice that carried clearly to where he stood, "I don't know if you can understand this, but in my own way I did love her."

Turning with a brisk wave, like a salute, she disappeared into the plane.

Brock stood and watched at the window until the plane took off, trying in vain to spot his mother's regal blond head in the row of tiny windows and waving once in a while just in case. Finally he turned to leave, relieved that his mission had been accomplished. He loved his mother, but he sure hoped that Hawaii knew how to handle her.

Joanna folded the road map haphazardly, stuffed it into the glove compartment and then settled back happily into her seat. She wasn't quite sure where they were, but they both liked it better that way. The sky was streaked with pink, and they planned to stop at the next decent place for dinner and then find a motel. Joanna was starving, but she was almost ready to skip the meal and head straight to the motel. She couldn't wait to be alone with Jack. In bed.

The day, beginning with the funeral and ending with her ugly confrontation with Kay, had been exhausting. It had taken Joanna a good couple of hours to shake the uneasiness the conversation with Kay had left her with. The lady was obviously insane, and she'd been living with her. But was it only that?

She turned and looked at Jack as he drove. Wearing a faded denim shirt and jeans, he looked relaxed and ruggedly handsome. Sensing her look, he turned and flashed a grin in her direction.

"How are you doing, honey? Getting tired?"

"A little, I guess. How about you? Do you want me to take a turn driving?"

"No. In fact, what I'd really like is to stop the car this instant in the middle of the road and make love to you. How does that sound?"

Playfully, Joanna snuggled over next to him and put her arms around his neck, burying her nose in his collar. That sounds just fine with me, Mr. Curtis, she thought to herself.

An hour and a half later, with two thick pan-fried steaks, baked potatoes, salad and a bottle of house red wine under their belts, they flopped on a motel bed, giddy with laughter, exhaustion and the wine.

Sobering suddenly, Jack turned to her, both hands on her waist, and looked intently into her eyes.

"It feels so good to be here with you, Joanna, to have you as my wife again."

"I know, Jack; I feel the same way. I can't quite believe it. I have to keep pinching myself."

Tipping her head up, he lowered his mouth and kissed her slowly, his tongue exploring the soft inner recesses of her mouth. Gradually the pressure increased, and his arms tightened around her. She snaked her arms up until they were clasped around his neck, and they lay side by side on the bed, their bodies pressed close.

Joanna thought dreamily of the days ahead. They planned to be gone a week. Seven full days of meandering on back roads, stopping in at out-of-the-way restaurants, making love whenever and wherever they pleased. She remembered how on their first honeymoon, on the island of Barbados, they'd made love on the beach under the stars. It had been the most perfect, most wonderful thing she'd ever experienced. Maybe this time they could try the woods. . . .

Joanna wondered why her mood had shifted suddenly, and then she realized that thinking about Barbados and the beach had made her remember Kay. Hawaii. Today was the day they were to have flown off together. In fact, if Kay was still going, her plane had probably just taken off.

Joanna imagined her sitting in her first-class aisle seat, imperiously ordering a very dry martini from the stewardess and waiting impatiently, annoyed at the service before giving it a chance.

Did any part of her wish she were there with Kay? she thought suddenly, then pushed the thought away. Of course not. Kay was out of her mind—and besides, she'd rather have a plain old motel and Jack any day of the week.

So what was bothering her all of a sudden? Was she still brooding over what Kay had said, her harsh criticism of her decision to remarry Jack? They were words Joanna had already said to herself, jokingly, a million times. Yeah, it was crazy to be marrying Jack again, but what the hell. . . .

Why was she paying any attention to the woman at all? Joanna shivered, and Jack held her more tightly, smoothing her back and nuzzling her ear.

The problem was, crazy though Kay might be, she *had* given her a lot. Even now, Joanna noticed the difference in herself. The clothes she had brought along, the loosely belted raw-silk pant suit she was wearing now, seemed almost incongruous with the homey, garish furnishings of the motel. Sure, this was fun, like old times, but didn't part of her miss the luxuries she'd grown used to? It wasn't as if she were suddenly turning up her nose and saying she was too good for a roadside steakhouse and a thirty-dollar-a-night motel or anything, but didn't it—if she was honest with herself—feel a little like slipping backward?

"Hey, baby, let's see if the shower works."

Jack bounced off the bed and started unbuttoning his shirt. For a moment, Joanna lay still, reluctant to abandon her train of thought. Then she shook herself. Jack was standing there with no shirt on, his tanned, muscular chest rising from the waistband of his jeans in a way that quickened her breathing.

What on earth was wrong with her? She had a man like Jack Curtis standing in front of her inviting her into the shower, and she was daydreaming about a life-style she hardly knew anything about. Well, maybe "hardly" wasn't quite the right word, she corrected herself. She'd had a taste. And if she knew herself at all, she'd find a way to get more. Right now, though, a motel shower with her new husband sounded pretty terrific.

Liz had wanted to stay and be with Stuart for a while after the funeral, so Jill and David left alone. David's eyes still weren't quite well enough for him to drive, so Jill got into the driver's seat. She found herself gripping the wheel nervously. Probably all the tensions of the day, she said to herself, the funeral, and making sure her mother was all right. Her mother seemed to be in better shape than she was, Jill thought ruefully. She'd looked so beautiful and strong, standing there talking to Stuart Brooks at the chapel, that it had made her want to weep.

What was wrong with her? Of course, she knew what was wrong. Why was she pretending? She had to ask David the truth, and she couldn't wait another second.

"David . . ." She turned to face him, then thought better of it. She would ask him when they got to her apartment. It would feel safer there, more private.

But when they arrived at her apartment and Jill went into her room to change out of her black dress, she realized that a different environment wasn't going to make what she had to do any easier. Calm down, she chided herself. Remember? This is David, the guy you love. What do you think you're going into, anyway, the Spanish Inquisition? You're just going to ask him to clear up a few things—ask him a couple of questions. That's all.

Pulling on a soft oversize shirt over her slacks, Jill brushed her hair, then dabbed cologne on her wrists. She knew she was stalling. It was time.

David was standing by the window, sipping a mug

of coffee, when she entered the living room. His face brightened when she walked in.

"I heated up some coffee. I don't know about you, but I really needed it."

"David . . ." Jill walked over and stood in front of him. "David, I need to ask you a couple of questions."

Seeing the serious look on her face, David's face creased in a worried frown.

"Jill, what is it, has something happened?"

"No . . . well, not exactly."

"Would you mind explaining that?" David's voice held an edge.

Jill walked to the other side of the room and began carefully adjusting books on the shelves so that all the bindings were even. Then, abruptly, she turned around to face him.

"David, there's been some vicious gossip about you going around Genoa City. I hate to even mention this to you, because I'm not usually one to listen to stories. But I can't help it. I have to know." She swallowed nervously.

The expression on David's face was unreadable. "Go on."

"Well, some people are saying that you had to leave the east coast . . . that you were involved in some kind of . . . of scandal. Something to do with the construction business. I didn't want to believe what I was hearing, but you've always been so vague about your life back east, and I didn't know . . . what to . . . think . . ." Her voice trailed off.

David sat still, not saying anything, his face impassive. Jill wanted to scream, "Say something! Don't just sit there!" What could he possibly think of her for listening to dirty, evil-minded gossip? What did it matter, even if it were true? She shouldn't have said anything. She should have trusted him. He'd said he had some stuff to work out. Maybe he would have told her in his own good time. . . . Her thoughts jumped wildly, trying to find something that made sense, something she could believe in. . . .

The next thing she knew, she was in David's arms, locked in an embrace so intense she thought her heart would stop.

"Oh, my poor darling Jill." He kissed her softly and then looked down at her, smiling. "This must have been driving you crazy."

Jill nodded, not trusting herself to speak.

David walked her over to the sofa and sat down with her, taking her hands in his. "I told you I had some things to take care of," he said. "Well, I probably should have told you everything then, but I didn't want to burden you. You've been through so much, what with your father and my operation. I just thought it wasn't the time to bring you in on something that has nothing to do with you."

He reached up to smooth a tendril of hair from her face, then continued, "Yes, there was a scandal of sorts back east, but it isn't what it sounds like. There was a mix-up, and my company's name got on some government list of construction companies accused of being involved in a big pay-off deal, falsifying contracts, that kind of thing. My name was in the papers a lot . . . that's probably where your spy got her information"—he smiled—"and I had to testify. I still have to go back east to appear in court a few more times until the hearings are completed. But I have a good lawyer, and I don't have anything to hide. And as for my moving out here, I was ready for a change of scenery anyway, and this mess seemed like as good a time as any to leave. I'd just broken up with a woman, too."

Jill's heart skipped a beat. "Go on," she said quietly.

"She was the woman you saw that day, the blonde, coming out of my room. She flew out here when she heard that I had to have an operation. Probably the only selfless act she's managed in her whole life." David spoke bitterly, with a hard edge to his voice that she'd never heard before.

"Oh, yes," he continued, staring past Jill and into the distance. "Janet was a prize. I thought I was in love with her, really in love. And then I discovered what the word 'greed' really meant. Janet was only interested in one thing. Money. I was making quite a bit through my construction business, and I was ready to cut out, maybe buy a house outside of New York City and start breeding horses—a dream I've always had. Well, suddenly Janet wanted no part of me. Once I no longer represented diamond trinkets, a private limo and a fat expense account—she just wasn't interested. And then when my name got linked up with the scandal—you've never seen someone in a dress run so fast. I think the only reason she came out here to visit me in the hospital was because she wanted to find out if she could keep on staying at the apartment she was living in. It's in a luxury building I happen to own, and I wasn't charging her any rent."

David paused, searching Jill's eyes. "Anyway, I think that's just about my entire slate—problems and all. I never meant to hide anything from you. I just didn't want to be a burden. Can you forgive me?" He looked at her pleadingly.

Jill felt as if a huge weight had been lifted from her

body. Suddenly she was as light as air and wonderfully free. She knew she should have trusted her instincts, trusted David, even when no one else did.

"Oh, David, I'm so sorry. Can *you* forgive *me?*"

The next moment she was in his arms, locked in an embrace she wanted never to end. A tremendous feeling of peace came over her. This was where she belonged. She didn't care whether David wore overalls and drove a pick-up truck, or if they spent the rest of their lives on a little farm hoeing corn and raising kids. This was the man she wanted. Forever.

"We're both forgiven, then," he said, pulling her to her feet and opening his arms. "Now, let's get down to really important business." Slowly he bent his head and claimed her mouth with his.

Liz Foster stood under a spreading shade tree watching as Stuart Brooks said good-bye to the last of his friends and family who had come to Jennifer's funeral. Again, she noted how tired he looked. He'd been so strong throughout all of this, she thought, so incredibly strong. For a moment she felt ashamed of herself, of her own weeks of giving up on the world after Bill had died—of hiding from the truth and trying to pretend that the bottom hadn't just fallen out of her world.

But it hadn't. Here she was, able to feel and enjoy the sun on her skin, the smell of the newly turned earth, the sadness of loss—and the bittersweet pleasure of going on.

The last limousine pulled away, and Stuart turned to her.

"Liz," he said simply. His voice was exhausted, but he sounded at peace, she thought. "Thank you for staying."

He walked toward her and took her hand, clasping it in both of his. "You know, it helped make me strong knowing you were here today. This morning I didn't think I'd have the willpower to get through it. But somehow you find reserves of strength you didn't know you had. Why don't we walk a little bit?"

Together they crossed the road and headed down a narrow tree-lined path leading away from the grave-yard. Liz stopped for a moment, balancing on Stuart's arm, and took off her shoes. She was going to ruin her stockings, but she didn't care. The earth felt good through her toes, damp and alive. She dug in her heels with each step, enjoying the cool sensation on the soles of her feet.

"Wait a minute, Stuart." They stopped again and Liz turned around to face him. "May I?" She stood on tiptoe and reached up to loosen his somber tie. "There, that's better."

"This is even better," he said, pulling the tie from around his neck and undoing the top buttons of his shirt. "Now maybe I can breathe again."

They both laughed, looking into each other's eyes, sharing their sadness, sharing their hope. If both of them hadn't lost their mates, thought Liz, they probably wouldn't be here, together, like this. But they both understood something now, something about dying, and about living. Having a loved one die didn't justify giving up and . . . well, dying along with them. You had to go on. Not just for yourself, or for your children—but for the one who had gone.

Bill and Jennifer had loved life, holding on to it with both hands and never letting go, no matter what kind of ride it tried to give them. Neither would have wanted their loved ones to just give up and crawl into a hole. Liz had tried that for a few weeks, and it hadn't worked.

No, the only way to fight the sadness and the pain was to keep on going, to keep searching. It was something she and Stuart both understood, without even talking about it. Let other people talk and whisper about her staying behind to be with Stuart after his wife's funeral. They were here now, together, feeling the sun, feeling the earth beneath their feet, laughing together, knowing that they were alive *for* the husband and the wife—the lovers—that they had just lost.

The most loving and respectful thing they could do in their memory was to go on living, and loving, as hard as they could.

Turning to Stuart, Liz grabbed hold of his hand and squeezed it hard, holding his eyes for a long moment.

"Life's still good, Stuart," she said simply. "Remember, you taught me that."

"I know. I'll try to remember. I still have my health and I've been blessed with four happy, healthy daughters. Thanks for reminding me." Stuart smiled down at her.

Together, Liz dangling her shoes from her fingers and Stuart his tie, they continued down the sun-dappled path to the field below.

Stuart's daughter Leslie brought her fists down on the piano keys. She couldn't get this particular section right no matter how she tried. She wasn't feeling well; her stomach felt queasy. For weeks she had dismissed it as being the flu, but she wasn't fooling herself for a minute.

Removing her hands carefully from the keyboard,

she clasped her fingers together so tightly that her knuckles became as white as the keys below. Eyes upward, she prayed. Oh, Lord, she cried out in her thoughts, I've never prayed before. I don't even know there is a Lord. But I have to hope that You can hear me. Lord, I have sinned. I am an adultress. I am carrying another man's child. I don't want to sin anymore, but please make this baby go away. It won't have a father, Lord. I can't tell Lance that our affair caused this to happen. It would destroy his marriage to my sister, and she would never forgive me. Please, Lord, please, I can't go on. Then she lowered her head to the ebony shelf and sobbed.

She knew some prayers were never answered.

COLUMBIA PICTURES
presents
YOUNG AND RESTLESS
Official Licensed Merchandise

For **FREE** brochure of all merchandise, send a self addressed, stamped, LEGAL size envelope to:

UPPYTRACKS

6513 Lankershim Blvd.
No. Hollywood, California 91606

Special Limited Offer to Soaps & Serials™ Readers!

ONLY $7.95!
plus Shipping & Handling

SAVE 25%!

The GIANT History Book of
DALLAS™

★ Relive the excitement of the complete Ewing Family Saga!

★ Hundreds of wonderful photos — many in full color!

★ *Special Discount* for Soaps & Serials™ readers! Save 25% off the cover price!

★ A unique collector's item for every *Dallas*™ fan!

★ More than 200 pages filled with the adventures of *J.R., Bobby, Miss Ellie, Jock, Sue Ellen, Pamela* and all your favorite characters!

★ Published by Doubleday/Dolphin

To get your copy of DALLAS,™ mail this coupon along with your check or money order for $9.90 (price includes $1.95 for shipping & handling) to: Soaps & Serials™, P.O. Box 5006, Rocky Hill, CT 06067.

Name _____

Street _____ Apt. No. _____

City _____ State _____ Zip _____

Telephone (area code) _____